The tank swung around, trying to run him down

Bolan jumped out of the way, then vaulted onto the bucking machine.

Despair seized him. He was on top of the tank but felt powerless—until he saw the bobbing cannon.

He grabbed the barrel at its base and pulled himself along with his hands and legs.

Suddenly the turret began to swivel. It jerked to the right, then to the left. The Executioner hung on, determined to keep from slipping.

A clap of thunder filled his ears and the metal grew hotter and hotter under his hands. The cannon had been fired.

They were trying to burn him off!

MACK BOLAN
The Executioner

DON PENDLETON's EXECUTIONER

MACK BOLAN

Cambodia Clash

A GOLD EAGLE BOOK FROM

W🌐RLDWIDE

TORONTO · NEW YORK · LONDON · PARIS
AMSTERDAM · STOCKHOLM · HAMBURG
ATHENS · MILAN · TOKYO · SYDNEY

First edition May 1984

ISBN 0-373-61065-3

Special thanks and acknowledgment to
Tom Jagninski for his contributions to this work.

Printed in Canada

"What is it that moves us as a race? Good times? Frolic? No, we move by challenge, by necessity, by hard times, by grinding need. The world is not a garden, and it never was. This earth is a crucible, from which the human race was formed and tempered and spit out to subdue a jungle whose law is not the survival of the fittest but of the vilest and most savage."

— *Mack Bolan*

Dedicated to Andrzej Konzaki, and to the paraplegic veterans of the Vietnam War.

PROLOGUE

From Mack Bolan's journal:

I was a member of the U.S. Army's Special Forces in Vietnam. I left the war for personal reasons. While I was there word had come to me that my family—that most revered, no, sacred unit of modern man—had been devoured by perverse elements back home. Driven by the same motivation that compelled me to enlist in my country's army, I felt I had no choice. I had to return home to avenge the desecration of my family.

Had this horrifying event not occurred, I would have served out my tour of duty. I never once questioned the war or my presence in Southeast Asia. When I enlisted it never entered my mind that I could dodge the draft and escape to Canada or opt for jail as a conscientious objector.

My country was at war. She needed me. I had to go. But little did I know, did anyone know, that our soldiers would spend ten thousand days engaged in what now seems like a futile exercise. I say futile because the number of casualties and lives lost on both sides could never be explained away. The cost in dollars—although astronomical—was secondary. I know there are those who would argue that it was not for nothing. Well, of those I would ask for an explanation of what was achieved.

Nothing was achieved. Witness the presence of the Communist regime in South Vietnam.

When U.S. fighting men returned home from the beaches of Normandy, from Guadalcanal and Corregidor at the end of the Second World War, there were ticker-tape parades and strewn confetti on the streets of almost every major metropolis. Young women and wives were hugging and kissing complete strangers—anyone in uniform—as they disembarked from aircraft carriers in New York Harbor and military transport planes in California airports.

Then, America was ecstatic. She was glad to have her sons back home.

But when the United States forces finally left Vietnam, the war did not actually end there. For the men who returned home, another, more personal battle was just beginning.

After America ended its involvement in the Southeast Asian conflict many veterans came home physically unscathed, but irreparably and psychologically wounded. Men in the prime of their youth left these shores, but only hollow-eyed shells returned. And it appeared as if there was no place for them in this society.

These beaten souls were not seeking recognition as heroes. All they wanted was to be accepted once more. They were seeking a place in society—a place that was rightfully theirs. A place that was categorically and unequivocally denied them. They were disoriented pariahs in an America that screamed for their help only years before.

It was damn near taboo for any Vietnam vet to talk about his experience. An exercise that would have, perhaps, exorcised some of the horrors and nightmares these men lived with constantly. But America did not want to know. These men had returned with indelible mental lesions to broken families.

I talked to a vet just yesterday. I visited him at a

psychiatric treatment center. With an armless sleeve he tried to brush away the tears that rolled down his cheeks onto the hospital gown. Then, as he shifted restlessly in his wheelchair he told me: "At times in the jungle I was so afraid that I came very close to running away, but I didn't. I stayed and fought. I was fighting for my country. Wasn't I? I know I'll never be the same again. Perhaps I'll have to spend the rest of my life in this place. I'm scared to go out there. But if I'm called up to fight again, I'll gladly go, if they would have me. I love America."

I love America. The land of the free and the home of the brave.

Yeah.

I was lucky. I was forced to leave behind in the scorched earth of Southeast Asia my sniper duty and the mental anguish that inevitably would have been visited upon me, as was the case with so many vets.

But I returned home to find another kind of jungle. The one in Vietnam seemed like an Iowan country fair compared to the evil that lurked in each concrete clearing, on every street corner in the cities of these United States.

This menace, while not new, had extended its claws to snatch my family, avariciously gobbling them up in its maw.

Since time began, man has stood in defense of his loved ones. I was too late to save mine. But I was determined to avenge them. And I knew my actions would be justified and exonerated, if not on earth, then by some higher order, on some other plane.

I was alone. I had no family. I had no friends.

But I did have a battle plan.

In thirty-eight blood-drenched campaigns, from the steel-and-glass jungle of Manhattan in the East to the windswept cliffs of Big Sur in the West, from the Caribbean basin to the Hawaiian islands, I penetrated their defenses, striking at them relentlessly, until they felt surrounded on every side.

It was total war.

Along the way I was hounded by the law, by government agencies. I was branded a butcher. These same groups, I think, secretly reveled in the notion that I was doing something good, but I was hunted in every quarter. Finally I was offered "amnesty," because the true meaning behind my activities could not be ignored.

Mile one.

I accepted the pardon on condition. I needed one more week because I felt I had unfinished business with the Mafia. With the help of Hal Brognola, an FBI agent who would later become a dear and trusted friend, I successfully struck at the remaining six centers of Mafia power. My second mile was now history.

Then, in a bogus accident in Central Park from which I escaped unhurt, I was given full government sanction, albeit covertly, and a new identity. So were born the Stony Man program and Colonel John Phoenix. I had entered my third mile and the Terrorist Wars.

Hal Brognola filled the necessary role as liaison between the White House and Stony Man Farm. There were others, too, like Andrzej Konzaki, my ace weaponsmith, Aaron "The Bear" Kurtzman, a computer wizard, the men of Able Team and Phoenix Force, and April. Dear April Rose.

During my odyssey, I had met many women and even loved a few. But none of them ever touched the plexus of my being like April. A brilliant, beautiful soul with whom I loved to share idyllic moments—moments when we were not fighting side by side in the killzone. She, like the other members of the Stony Man group, had become my family.

I admired her utter dedication to the Phoenix program and her uncomplaining alliance with me. I know there were many times when she must have thought of marriage and the "normal" life. But she, more than any other, knew the path I had chosen.

I sometimes think that I failed April. But then again I believe she understood. I am sure that those who met April grieve with me. They say time is the greatest healer. I wonder. How does one come to terms with the pain of a sacrifice such as this?

Goodbye, my love.

Soon after the attack on Stony Man Farm, in which April was killed, I was asked to go to a Russian satellite country. The purpose of this trip, I was told, was to chaperone the daughter of a long-time friend from my Vietnam days, Brig.-Gen. James Crawford. She was invited to take part in an invitational sports meet there.

What was supposed to be some R&R turned out to be a mission of no less importance than any I had undertaken before. In fact, I came face to face with an enemy perhaps more deadly than any other. The KGB had conceived a brilliant plan, using a double, to frame me for the murder of a worker party leader.

In that mission I encountered evil in its purest form. Evil that manifested itself in terrorism, subversion, oppression, murder and "wet affairs." Wet as in bloody.

In the Soviet Union terror is a way of life. Unlike the Mafia the motivation is not money, but world domination. And this oppression would be achieved at any cost. Men have made terror a daily business. Each new day is spent devising ways to infiltrate vulnerable nations, especially unsuspecting ones in the Third World like Grenada, under the guise of economic aid. The ulterior motive, of course, is to create a Communist beachhead, in close juxtaposition to the U.S.—a staging area to export terror and subversion.

I returned home from Russia with a masterlist of KGB operatives. My duty was to hand it over to the government authorities, but it was my insurance until I found the highly placed sleeper mole who had masterminded the assault on Stony Man Farm. I found him and I liquidated him in the White House—in front of the President of the United States.

I was now beyond sanction.

I had come full circle.

Once again I would tread the paths of a shadow world.

Someone once said: There is no army as mighty as an idea whose time has come.

I, The Executioner, have arrived. Out of the shadows I have emerged, my presence well defined.

Let them beware—the procurers of flesh who would prey on vulnerable young girls in empty bus terminals; the purveyors of the white powdered death who lurk in school-yards, pouncing on the innocent; the exporters of terror who would try to steal our freedom.

Let the scum beware—those propelled by base urges and the tantalizing prospect of filthy lucre.

I do not judge them. No, the laws of mankind were laid down long ago.

I am their judgment.

I am their scourge.

I am The Executioner.

Of those who have followed my movements from the beginning of the Mafia Wars through my Phoenix phase, I'm sure there are many who question my motives.

Who is this self-appointed warrior? you ask. His strikes against the Mob were justified. Sure. But is he any longer necessary? After all, we do have law-enforcement agencies and military organizations to protect our way of life.

Well, let me answer this way: If you could dispassionately look at the hypodermic-riddled arm of your daughter's corpse and *not* ask, "Where did I fail?"; if you attend church and not pray for peace because you believe all is well with the world, then that is the day I need be no more.

You did not fail. Animal Man succeeded.

I must continue the fight for freedom. Return it to those from whom it was taken away, whether they are civilians or POWs. This is why I am on my way to Cambodia.

1

Brilliant bolts of lightning split the night sky. Mack Bolan's flesh crawled as he paddled faster. If the storm caught them, their dinghies would overturn on the first big wave. He glanced over his shoulder to see how Eng, his Khmer Rouge guide, was doing. She was paddling the second dinghy. Although the night was dark he could make out her position by the phosphorescent glow each time her paddle dipped in the water. It was a natural phenomenon for which the sea off the coast of Cambodia was famous— because of a high phosphorus content, the sea glowed when stirred.

Bolan could tell Eng was lagging, and he cursed himself for not ensuring that the dinghies had been tied together. He had mentioned the idea to the captain of the smuggling junk soon after they put out to sea from Thailand, but at journey's end nothing was done. By then it was too late to do anything, the captain insisting they disembark immediately so he could head back before a Vietnamese gunboat showed up.

The thought that he might make it while she perished gnawed at Bolan. Not that he was responsible for her; officially she was in command of the infiltration. And he had warned her. Back on the junk he had suggested that because of the storm they should abort the water route, go back to Thailand and try crossing into Cambodia by land.

In return he received a patronizing, "In war, Colonel, one must take risks." A lesson for the Executioner from a nineteen-year-old know-it-all. But that was precisely the point: since she was only nineteen, he felt responsible for her.

"Paddle faster," he shouted.

A rumble traveled through the sky and a gust of wind blew in his face, the first of the night. The water, calm as a pond until then, rippled in the freshening breeze. On shore, the Khmer Rouge reception committee was flashing a torch to give him a bearing. The light was moving to his left, telling him he was being carried off course by the current. But he made no attempt to correct this. He would worry about meeting them later.

Right now the important thing was to reach shallow water. If his dinghy overturned in the deep, he would go down like a stone. In addition to his battle gear, Bolan's money belt was loaded with gold dollars, money to start a rescue operation if the report of American POWs proved true.

The rumbling in the sky grew louder and more frequent. Bolan felt a raindrop. Suddenly a dazzling bolt zigzagged ahead and the wind picked up with a vengeance. On the beach, palm trees swayed wildly and clouds of sand blew out to sea. The water turned choppy. Soon there were great swells. Bolan's strokes became frantic. He glanced over his shoulder. Eng, too, was paddling furiously. They were racing against the storm.

A wall of water caught them from behind. Bolan felt himself being lifted into the air. With a foaming roar, the dinghy and its passenger spilled onto the shallows. Before Bolan had time to recover, the undertow receded, sucking him back into the sea, his face and hands scraping the sandy bottom. When he finally surfaced, coughing and spitting, he was back where the water had picked him up, feet touching ground but up to his neck in water.

Eng! He looked around for his guide. The next moment he forgot all about her, forced to concentrate on his own survival as a breaking wave buried him. The crashing waves propelled him forward, the seafloor sliding from under his feet. His training in the Seals came in handy. As a Green Beret he took part in several exchange programs with the Seals, the Navy's special forces.

In the Seals, almost every aspect of marine combat and survival skills are taught. Bolan was always impressed by this branch of the armed forces and enjoyed the exchange programs in which he took part. As a Green Beret he had been amazed at the specialized equipment that was constantly being developed by the Navy.

Now, his thoughts kept returning to his last underwater hit in the Atlantic, just before the attack on Stony Man Farm in which April was killed. On that mission, he had agreed to try out the Navy's ELF—extremely low frequency—a highly advanced form of radio transmission that was the latest top-secret development in submarine communication.

Deafened by the pounding waves, blinded by sheets of rain, slipping and falling, Bolan swam-walked to shore. And he did it with every bit of his equipment intact, Beretta on his back, gold dollars around his waist.

In the next instant, however, he had shed it all: gun, gold, haversack, boots. Fifty yards from shore, illuminated by the flickering light of the storm, rising and falling amid the turbulent ocean, he saw Eng clinging to her overturned dinghy. He ran back into the sea and struck out in her direction.

What followed was something out of a nightmare. Arms flailing, his body tossed this way and that, Bolan gulped water, straining to keep her in view as he fought his way through the waves. And all the time he kept thinking that it might be for nothing. The thought kept nagging him that even if he did reach her he would never make it back because the undertow was pulling her farther and farther out.

Finally he reached her, only to discover that she did not know how to swim.

Now began a second fight with the storm, but somehow this one was easier, perhaps because it was merely physical; the mental strain, the fear of not getting to her or losing her, was gone. They let the dinghy go because it was only acting as a wind drag, and set out for shore with her on his back. He was doing the breaststroke, riding the waves, occasionally going under when a wave was too big.

For a nonswimmer her calm was outstanding. She lay on his back, hands clutching his shirt collar, a position that was taboo in any Red Cross lifesaving course. But it was the only possible position under the circumstances. This way she could anticipate the waves, close her mouth in time and press closer to him to present less resistance each time he went under a wave.

It took them forty minutes to get to shore. Although the storm had passed soon after they started out, the sea continued to be turbulent. Once again he realized that the current had carried him off course. Their legs found the sand some two hundred yards from where he had left his gear.

In Bolan's absence a firefight had broken out, and tracer bullets were flying about where he had stowed his equipment. The sight sent his adrenaline pumping and cleared his brain of fatigue. It was obvious that the fighting was over his money. If it was stolen, the mission would be a washout. He grabbed Eng's hand, and they ran for the cover of the palms.

"Who are they?" he shouted over the crashing of waves as they crouched behind a tree and watched the fireworks.

"Moulaka, I think," she replied. "Capitalist guerrillas. They fight the Vietnamese, but they fight us, too."

"Are they connected with Khmer Serei?"

"Same. We call them Moulaka."

Now he knew who they were, a rival resistance movement backed by the U.S. His mind raced. Somehow he had to put an end to this fight. If Moulaka won, he would never see his money.

"Give me your gun," he said.

"No! I will go."

"Your gun," he repeated, gripping her by the elbow, preventing her from rising. At his touch, her eyes flared with anger. In the Orient a man did not touch a woman. But she made no reference to his touching her.

"I am still the commander," she said.

"Then behave like one," he retorted. "A commander gives orders but leaves the fighting to soldiers."

For a moment she hesitated, rattled by the novelty of the argument. She handed him the gun.

"And the magazines."

Dutifully she reached into her pockets and gave him four 20-round clips. "What are you going to do?"

"I'll see when I get there."

He ran in a crouch, keeping to the shadows. By now the sky had partly cleared and there were periods of moonlight. Eng's gun was a Skorpion, one of the lightest machine pistols made. It weighed only three-and-a-half pounds. A Czech invention, this one had been made for the French secret service. He could tell by the letter F stamped on the grip. He wondered what she was doing with such a weapon. Or were the French now backing the Khmer Rouge as well? It would not surprise him. A lot of people had a finger in the Cambodian pie, with its prospects of offshore oil.

The U.S. was backing Prince Sihanouk's Moulaka, the Chinese were supporting Pol Pot's Khmer Rouge, while the Soviets—through the good graces of the Vietnamese— were backing Samrin's puppet government.

As Bolan neared the fighting, he observed that it had degenerated into positional warfare, with men taking potshots at one another from behind palms. From the sound of things, Moulaka, on the side nearest to him, were shooting American-supplied M-16s. The others were using Type 68s, a Chinese weapon. When he got close enough, Bolan dropped behind a palm for a quick recon. He could attack Moulaka from behind, but such a maneuver would not necessarily win the battle. Without an avenue of escape, they would be forced to take him on face to face. And they could do this without much worry. Judging from the flashes, they outnumbered the Khmer Rouge two to one.

No, he must attack in such a way that they could and *would* run. The question was how to make two dozen men retreat. He worked his way inland, then around the side, coming out at a point between the warring parties, but well out of their way. On his right were the Khmer Rouge, on his left Moulaka and straight ahead a stretch of open ground at the end of which sat his gear.

Bolan pulled out the butt on the Skorpion and waited for a lull in the shooting. One came a minute or two later. He took a deep breath and shouted in Vietnamese, "Open fire!'' Then he began shooting, darting from tree to tree to make it look as if he were many people, firing in the direction of both Moulaka and Khmer Rouge. Both sides opened up on him. The ruse was working. The muzzle-flashes were moving away in both directions, each group withdrawing while covering itself with gunfire. ''Cease fire!'' Bolan shouted in Vietnamese before anyone would tell that only one man was attacking. ''Cease fire!'' He cupped his hands. ''Bandits, surrender. You will be treated as prisoners of war.''

A scatter of bursts answered this well-known lie. Then all was silent, except for the crashing of waves. The moon came out, illuminating the beach with a silvery sheen. There wasn't a soul in sight. The combatants had fled in the face of a common enemy, an enemy not known for foolish bravado. If the enemy attacked, it meant it had the muscle power to go with it.

Bolan waited until a cloud hid the moon, then he ran to the water's edge and collected his gear. As he made his way back, he fired sporadic bursts into the trees in case the Moulaka got any ideas about returning.

Eng was waiting for him where he'd left her. ''You have the money?'' she asked.

''All here,'' he replied, tapping his belt.

''You checked?''

She was right. Someone might had tampered with it, substituting stones or Cambodian riels. He unzipped the belt, brought out one of the coins and stepped into the moonlight. In his palm glinted a twenty-dollar gold Double Eagle.

The mission was on.

AFTER A TWO-DAY TREK they arrived at the guerrilla base. It was basically a village, a conglomeration of long houses and huts on stilts with thatched roofs situated in a valley. The buildings surrounded a terra-cotta parade square with a pole that flew the flag of the Khmer Rouge.

As Bolan followed Eng past wandering dogs and crowing roosters, he observed that the villagers were a mixture of lowlanders and hill people. Once they would have had nothing to do with one another. The lowlanders considered the hill people savages. But war made for strange bedfellows as his own presence in the village testified.

From open doorways, women with children in their arms greeted him with curtsies. On the parade ground, guerrillas practicing bayonet combat paused to present arms.

Bolan wondered to what he owed these honors. Was it the gold he was bringing? Or his age? Everyone looked so young, at most in their early twenties. Forty years of war, disease and starvation had left Cambodia a country of children.

A young man in a camouflage beret emerged from a long house bristling with antennas. He hurried up to them, saluted and started speaking to Eng in Khmer, a language Bolan did not understand. With Eng, Bolan had communicated in English or Vietnamese or French.

The man had a long nail on one little finger, the sign of an intellectual. But he was a fighting intellectual. On his hip hung a Tokarev and around his neck he wore a necklace of what looked like shriveled dates. They were ears of the enemies he had killed.

The conversation over, Eng spoke to Bolan. "He will take you to your quarters." Then without a word she walked away.

"Thanks for your help," Bolan called after her, but she ignored him. He turned to the man. "Mack Bolan," he said, holding out his hand.

"Lieutenant P'um," he replied, taking it. Like Eng, the man struck Bolan as reserved and serious—the seriousness of revolutionary youth.

The two men made their way to the other side of the village. Bolan was the center of attention. For most of the inhabitants, he was their first glimpse of a white man, that race of giants their forefathers had driven out of the country. At least that's what the new history books said.

"Which tribe are the Montagnards?" Bolan asked. "In my day you could tell tribes by their costumes."

"The days of folklore are over," P'um said. "A pity perhaps, but that is life, is it not?"

Yeah, thought Bolan. That's life under Communism all right. Color gave way to drabness, individualism to regimentation, spontaneity to dialectics. And what was it all for? He had yet to see a Communist country that.... Bolan dismissed the thought. He did not come to Cambodia to fight the Vietnam War again; he had come to save Americans from a POW camp, and if these Communists were willing to help, good. He would need help.

P'um stopped in front of the hut that was to be Bolan's home, a one-room abode on stilts with a bamboo floor, mat walls and flaps for windows. On the ground, laid out on a sleeping mat, were a T-shirt, some rubber flip-flops and a *sampot*, a wraparound skirt.

He changed into them, retaining only his money belt, and followed P'um to the bathhouse, an enclosure with a big drum of water and a pail.

Bolan had a quick wash, then as he was about to shave he noticed P'um lingering nearby. Bolan asked the lieutenant to hold the mirror for him. In the next few minutes the ice between them broke, P'um's reserve giving way to curiosity over Bolan's pivoting-head razor. By the time they returned to the hut, Bolan knew quite a bit about the second-in-command of the base.

But it was the number one who interested him more. "Who is the commander?" he asked.

"Captain Macdok."

"When can I see him?"

"Now. Captain Macdok is waiting to eat with you."

"Let's go then."

They walked back to the center of the village, Bolan's rubber sandals flopping. He wore the T-shirt and the wrap-around skirt. His black fighter's suit had been taken away to be washed. As they approached the parade square, Bolan heard a commotion.

"What's going on there?" Bolan asked. He could see some angry villagers trying to attack a group of people being escorted by a squad of soldiers.

"The traitor and his family," P'um said.

"What traitor?"

"The man who told Moulaka you were arriving with gold. He was a spy."

"The reception committee returned?" Bolan asked.

"Last night. They had one dead and four wounded. That was a clever trick, Mr. Bolan. Everyone thought you were the Vietnamese."

Bolan and P'um stepped off the path to let the group pass. There was a man, two women and four children. The man had his wrists bound and the women were sobbing.

"What's going to happen to them?" Bolan asked after the group had passed.

"They will all be shot."

"The children, too?"

"The commander has ordered they should all die," P'um said. "As an example to others."

They came to the commander's hut. A guard went in to announce Bolan's arrival. The sentry then came out and motioned for Bolan to follow him.

"I will leave you here," P'um said. "If you need me I will be in the command post. The long house with the antennas."

Bolan lifted the corner of his *sampot* and climbed the steps. He entered a room that was similar to his, except larger. On a cloth on the floor was an array of dishes behind which sat the commander of the base, a frangipani in her freshly washed hair.

"Please sit down, Mr. Bolan," Eng said.

2

"So that's who they were saluting," Bolan said. He sat on the floor and added with a smile, "I thought it was me." Eng did not return the smile. "Why the big mystery?" he continued. "You could have told me from the start."

"A precaution," she replied. "We might have been captured. It was better for me that you not know who I am. Please," she said, motioning him to begin.

Bolan leaned over a bowl of sticky rice, took a handful and mashed it into a ball. He dipped it into some *prahoc*, the common Cambodian fish paste. "How long have you been in command?" he asked.

"A year."

"How big is your maquis?"

"Sixty men and women. Forty live in the village, the others in town."

"And what does the maquis do?"

"We raid Vietnamese convoys. Do you wish me to tell you about the prisoner-of-war camp?"

"Yes."

"The camp is in a fort," she began, "an old fort built by the French early in the century. It is on the coast. We don't know the exact number of prisoners. About two hundred."

"The League of Families said there were thirty," Bolan said.

"Thirty Americans. There are others. South Koreans, Thais, Filipinos, soldiers who fought for America against the revolution in Vietnam. There are also some Chinese and some Frenchmen. We do not know who the Frenchmen are. We think they are agents of the Central Intelligence Agency. After liberation, Americans sent agents into Vietnam."

"Why is this camp in Cambodia?"

"We do not know. I have made arrangements for you to see the fort tomorrow. You will go by truck. You will drive by the fort."

"I have to do a little more than that," said Bolan. "The League of Families insists that I establish for myself the presence of American prisoners there before I pay you a dime. I have to go inside."

"Do you not trust us?"

"Nothing to do with me, Eng. I'm simply following instructions. A lot of these organizations have had their fingers burned lately. All sorts of people from all kinds of resistance groups claim to have seen American POWs. To date they have all turned out to be ploys to make money. You can't blame the League for being cautious." He helped himself to a slice of dried fish. "You are not eating," he observed.

Eng took a chicken wing and bit into it daintily. "You do not need to go inside the fort," she said between bites. "You will be able to see them when they go to work. Every morning they leave the fort to walk to a mine. The prisoners work in a uranium mine."

"It's more complicated than that," Bolan said. "I have to speak to them, find out who they are. I have to take pictures and voice recordings. The League wants all that so they can convince the U.S. government of the existence of the camp. Right now the American government refuses to believe there are POWs in Cambodia.''

"How can you take pictures inside a camp?"

"I have a miniature camera. I also have a miniature tape recorder. Can you help me get inside the fort?"

"To enter the fort will be difficult. And expensive."

"I am authorized by the League to pay you whatever it costs to get me in there." He unzipped the money belt and brought out three Double Eagles. "Here's two thousand dollars to start."

Eng took the coins and rose to examine them by the light of the window. "Nineteen hundred and thirty three," she observed.

"The last year regular gold coins were minted in the United States. Why did you ask for coins?"

"The Chinese prefer coins to ingot."

"The Chinese?"

"Our fraternal brothers require that we pay in gold for the weapons they sell us," she said. "Who is the woman on the face?"

"Liberty."

"Who is Liberty?"

"A sort of American Marianne," said Bolan, referring to the symbol of the French republic. Eng would understand the comparison. Bolan had learned from P'um that she'd been educated in France.

In the course of Bolan's shave, P'um had told him he and Eng were children of the wilderness, as the Cambodians called children born out of wedlock to guerrillas. Raised in an orphanage, both had exhibited high intelligence and were sent by the party to study abroad, Eng to France and P'um to China.

"And this is two thousand dollars?" Eng asked.

"It's more than that. Each coin is worth over seven hundred dollars, two months ago anyway. Now it's probably higher."

A burst of gunfire echoed in the hills, followed by another and another. "One traitor less," said Eng, getting up to look out the window.

"Is it necessary to shoot children?" he asked.

"War is not a tea party, Mr. Bolan."

"But children?"

"When you do not have B-52s to terrorize your enemy into submission, you shoot children," she said quietly turning to face him. "Do you speak German?"

"No."

"A pity. Every month East Germans come from Phnom Penh to check the machines in the mine. You could have impersonated one of the technicians."

They were interrupted by a guard who entered and saluted. "*Envoyé.*" He stepped aside and a dust-covered courier in riding boots walked in, a dispatch case over his shoulder. He took out a scroll and handed it to Eng to read.

P'um arrived. Eng passed him the message and there began a long conversation in Khmer. Bolan could tell the discussion involved him because both kept glancing in his direction.

Finally Eng turned to him. "Do you speak Russian by any chance, Mr. Bolan?"

"Yes," he replied.

"Do you speak it well?"

"Why?"

"We think an opportunity has arisen to get you inside the fort," Eng said.

"But first we have to kill a Russian," P'um added.

BOLAN AWAITED THE arrival of his victim in sweltering heat. He was kneeling behind a boulder on the side of a hill, Beretta in a shoulder rig, binoculars in hand. His fighter's suit was drenched in sweat; it was midday and there was little cover from the blazing sun.

The Russian would be coming along the road that skirted the base of the hill. On the far side was a forest that hid the ambush party. Bolan chose his position on the rise so he could give the guerrillas plenty of warning.

Eng knelt by Bolan's side, in a black pajama suit and wide-brimmed bush hat. The Skorpion machine pistol was slung across her back.

A faint dust cloud rose in the distance. Bolan raised his binoculars. It was only a bus.

The road, a two-way dirt track, was the main coastal highway. They had seen many army trucks—Zils and Urals mainly—a few buses, the odd private car, scooters, motorcycles and an ox cart, but there was no sign of the Russian's car. According to the message he was riding a Gaz, a Soviet-made jeep.

The message identified the Russian as Major Karkor, newly appointed deputy chief of the KGB station in Hanoi, making his first tour of Cambodia. Bolan would have to get more information on the man before killing him. The important thing was that no one knew what he looked like.

A Russian would have no trouble getting into the POW camp. He could simply say he was curious and everyone would jump. It was thanks to Russian aid that Vietnam could afford to fight a war in Cambodia. Bolan would impersonate the Russian.

The bus roared by, its rooftop passengers playing dice. Then the countryside reverted to its hot silence. Bolan glanced at his watch. Karkor should have been here hours ago; he was due to resume his trip in the morning. They could not have missed him; they had been there since dawn.

"Maybe he's taken another route," Bolan muttered.

"This is the only road they travel," Eng said. "The small roads are too easy to ambush."

Bolan passed a sleeve across his damp forehead and looked up at the cloudless sky. He brought out his water bottle, drank from it and passed it to Eng, who took a small swig.

In the distance dust rose once more. Another bus? Bolan brought the field glasses up. This time it was something smaller. "The Gaz," he said.

"Is the Russian in it?"

Bolan zeroed in on the occupants. A Vietnamese soldier wearing a green pith helmet was in the driver's seat. A white man in a safari suit sat in the back. Next to him was an Oriental woman. "That's him," Bolan said. He swiveled and swept the other end of the road with his glasses. There was no oncoming traffic. "Block the road."

Eng blew a whistle and guerrillas ran out of the forest carrying logs. They made a barrier across the road, then dashed back into the woods. A curve in the road hid the roadblock from the approaching vehicle. The driver would have no time to turn the jeep around.

"There's an Oriental woman with him," Bolan said.

"An interpreter perhaps," she replied.

Bolan kept the glasses trained on the Russian. He was a big man with a curly beard and a shock of red hair. He sat sideways, engrossed in conversation with the woman, gesticulating constantly.

"You have the handcuffs?" Eng asked.

"Yes," Bolan said, tapping a pocket.

The jeep sped toward them and soon they could hear its engine. Bolan let the binoculars hang from its strap and brought up his Beretta. Eng did the same with her Skorpion.

The Gaz rounded the bend and came to a screeching halt at the barricade. An overanxious guerrilla stepped onto the road with his gun and the driver raised his hands. Then everything went wrong.

Instead of raising his hands as well, the Russian tossed a grenade. The Khmer Rouge fighter pulled the trigger. The grenade did not explode, but the burst did its work, blowing away half the woman's face. A scream of rage escaped the Russian's lips as he jumped out of the vehicle and charged the trigger-happy gunman.

The scene was so unexpected it left the rest of the ambush party rooted in their tracks. The Russian ignored the others to avenge the death of the woman. The strange sight of the man holding his weapon like a club instead of shooting, had everyone hypnotized, including the man who had fired.

The KGB agent reached the dumbstruck guerrilla and with a bellow proceeded to club him. The man went down and still the Russian continued to batter him. Suddenly the major noticed Bolan bearing down on him from the hill. The sight of another white man brought him to his senses and sent him running into the forest.

"Get the jeep off the road," Bolan shouted as he went in pursuit of the Russian.

A few guerrillas also took up the chase, but they soon fell back, unable to keep pace. Twice Karkor turned and fired, twice Bolan threw himself sideways. These moves increased the distance between them. The terrain thickened and Bolan no longer had visual contact with his quarry. Bolan could only follow by sound. Then there was silence.

A moment later Bolan discovered the reason. Before him was a slimy pond full of partially submerged logs. On the edge was a footprint. The Russian had gone into the pond and was hiding somewhere among those logs. Now it was the Soviet who lay in ambush.

Bolan dropped to one knee, eyes probing the gloom. The pond was in a depression and there was little light. Was it his imagination or was there a pair of eyes staring at him?

Bolan sprang for cover behind a tree. He raised his Beretta, and fired a burst, aiming to the side of his target. He did not want to kill Karkor, at least not yet, not before he found out why he had come.

The bullets thudded into the logs. "Give up," Bolan called out in Russian. "I know you're there."

For a moment there was silence, then from behind the logs a voice asked, "What do you want from me?"

"I only want to talk to you."

"Talk."

"Show yourself first."

Bolan heard the sound of something moving through the water.

Bolan realized Karkor was making his way out while distracting him with conversation. Bolan tossed a grenade, again aiming to the side. The explosion showered the area with wet mud. A full-throated scream rose from the logs, followed by splashing and gurgling.

A real actor, Bolan thought. But the stage direction was lousy, the scream too far from where the grenade had exploded. Concussion waves did not travel that far.

Bolan peered into the gloom, eyes smarting from sweat. Occasionally bubbles rose to the surface of the water, gas from decaying vegetation.

Suddenly a loud splash disrupted the pond's silence.

Before Bolan could react, Karkor was off and away through the bushes. Bolan skirted the edge of the pond and took off after him. The two men crashed through the bushes, thorns tearing at their clothes, branches whipping their faces.

The undulating terrain flattened out. Bolan began to catch up. Karkor's underwater swim had left him short of breath.

As they crossed a clearing, Karkor turned to shoot, but the weapon jammed.

Desperately running on, Karkor tripped over a vine and fell. By the time he raised himself on all fours, Bolan stood over him.

Karkor looked up, panting. He lowered his head as if to regain his breath, then lunged at Bolan.

Bolan sidestepped and brought the gun to the side of Karkor's head. The Russian collapsed in a wet heap. Bolan jerked the Russian's hands behind him, then snapped on the cuffs.

"Get up," he ordered, pulling Karkor by his jacket collar.

The man rose unsteadily to his feet.

"Now we talk," Bolan grated, prodding him with the Beretta.

"You won't learn anything from me."

"You'd be surprised."

Bolan retraced their route to the pond and pushed Karkor against a tree. "What is the purpose of your trip to Yen Sai?"

The man remained silent.

"Suit yourself," Bolan said. He holstered the Beretta. "On your knees."

Karkor did not move.

A left hook to the stomach doubled Karkor, a right to the head sent him to the ground. Bolan grabbed him by the jacket collar and dragged him over the mud into the slimy water. They thrashed about, Karkor cursing, Bolan trying to keep him down.

Karkor was fighting with renewed fury, fueled by the instinct for self-preservation. He wriggled and turned and kicked, and it took all of Bolan's strength to keep him submerged.

Bolan grabbed a handful of the man's hair and heaved him from the slime. He came up, coughing, gasping for air.

"The purpose of your trip to Yen Sai?" Bolan repeated.

"Go to hell."

Bolan lifted Karkor by the collar and dragged him back into the pond. This time he continued pressing him down even when bubbles rose. Karkor fought for his life, jerking his head, his whole body struggling.

The body slackened and Bolan pulled him to shore. Water gushed from Karkor's mouth and he vomited. Gasping, wheezing, his body struggled to replenish the oxygen supply, the yellow vomit forming a pool about his head.

When he had partially recovered, Bolan knelt by his side.

"No more, please. You killed my wife," Karkor grunted, weakly.

Bolan pulled him into a sitting position.

"While you and I fight our little war, your wife lies waiting to be buried. Why are you going to Yen Sai?" Bolan asked once more.

"To visit the POW camp." Karkor's voice was flat, sad.

"What for?"

"We want to increase production in the mine."

"What connection has the KGB got to the mine?"

"It is ours."

Now that was something, Bolan thought, a Cambodian gulag. The KGB, which supervised the concentration camps and the slave mines in Russia, was going international.

"How are you going to increase production?" he asked.

"We will bring in more workers from a POW camp in Laos."

"Americans?"

"Yes."

"How long did you intend to stay in Yen Sai?"

"A day. Not even that."

"Where will you stay?"

"At the town's hotel. What will you do with me?"

Bolan shrugged. "Haven't decided."

"What did you come for?" Karkor asked. "Why did you stop me?"

"To rescue the American prisoners in the Yen Sai camp."

"You are a crazy American. Have you seen the camp? It's a fortress. I don't understand why your government refuses to pay up. It's got the money."

"Pay up?" Bolan asked.

"The ransom money."

There were several hundred American servicemen still being held prisoner in Indochina. And Washington knew about it. They knew because Hanoi had sent a complete list. But the officials in Washington were pretending they did not know because they would not pay the fifty billion dollars in war reparation that Vietnam demanded for the prisoners' release.

A snapping twig announced the arrival of Eng and her guerrillas.

"We must go," she said.

Bolan turned his head for one split second and Karkor bolted.

Bolan unleashed one shot in a bullet to the brain.

3

Dusk was falling on the Cambodian landscape as they drove into Yen Sai, a small town with shady trees and unpaved streets. They drove slowly amid cyclists and water-buffalo carts on a street lined with dilapidated office buildings and villas, some protected by sandbags and barbed wire.

The place reminded Bolan of similar urban settlements during the Vietnam War: run-down, dusty, smelly. The same peeling walls, the same grass-sprouting sidewalks, the same stench of sewage from broken drains.

They passed an office building with a balcony where a red flag with a yellow star fluttered, the flag of Vietnam. The entrance was protected by sandbags and flanked by guard booths where Vietnamese soldiers stood with AKMs over their shoulders. They wore green fatigues and pith helmets with red stars, the same kind of uniform as P'um was now wearing at the wheel of the Gaz.

"What's in that building?" Bolan asked Eng.

"The headquarters of the 6th Mountain Battalion," she said. "They provide the troops for the garrison at the prisoner-of-war camp."

"And that?" He nodded in the direction of a villa that also flew a Vietnamese flag.

"The residence of the military governor," Eng said.

The jeep approached a park set behind a wall. They drove around it and came to a large mansion, the hotel.

They got out of the Gaz and went inside. P'um was left to carry the bags. People dressed in fine clothing were milling around the foyer. The sounds of dance music floated softly on the evening air.

Bolan's insides stirred uneasily. A good third of the faces were white. And they were Russians.

At the sight of Bolan a number of heads bowed. Bolan wore Karkor's KGB uniform. Eng wore an *ao dai*, a gaily-printed, flowing robe with trousers to match.

Bolan saluted, and they moved toward the registration desk. "Major and Madame Karkor," Eng said. "We have a reservation."

The clerk asked for their passports. Bolan reached into a pocket, frowned, tapped the other pockets, then snapped his fingers.

"I left them in the safari suit," he said in Russian. He turned to Eng. "Tell him we'll bring them down with us on our way to dinner."

Eng did not understand Russian, but they had practiced this scene in the Gaz, so she knew what to say. The clerk nódded that this would be perfectly all right, then asked Bolan to surrender his weapon.

"My gun?" Bolan said. He had not expected this.

"House rules, Major," a voice behind him said in Russian. "When there's drinking, everyone parks his weapon."

Bolan turned around. "Thank you, comrade." He handed in Karkor's AK-47 and the bandolier with the ammunition magazines. The clerk gave him a receipt.

A houseboy led them to their suite, then he turned on the ceiling fans, unrolled the mosquito netting over the double bed and showed Eng the phone and bathroom. She tipped him and he left.

While Eng unpacked, Bolan and P'um checked the rooms for listening devices. The Vietnamese were known to have no compunction about spying on their allies. But they found no bugs.

"The reception downstairs is a wedding," Eng told Bolan. "A Russian economics official married a Cambodian girl. The houseboy told me."

Bolan opened his Agfa camera and took out the spool. He gave it to P'um, plus the documents that were to be forged with the photos on the film: three passports, three IDs and three driving licenses. They had taken pictures of one another earlier in the day.

"Tell Keysone we need the passports in an hour," Eng said to her second-in-command. "Also your driving license. You will have to show that when you book into your hotel." P'um would stay in a hotel for enlisted men.

Bolan went into the sitting room, lit a cigarette and perused some papers they had found in Karkor's briefcase while Eng showered. The papers were background material relating to the mine.

A knock on the door interrupted him. He opened it to face a Tartar giant in a badly cut suit, eyes slightly bloodshot from too much liquor.

The man spoke. "Excuse me, I thought this was Major Karkor's suite."

"Come in," Bolan said. He closed the door behind the visitor and motioned him to a chair. "What can I do for you?"

"You're Major Karkor?" said the other.

"One of them," said Bolan. "The one you're referring to is my cousin."

"But . . . Yuri's cousin is dead."

"I'm the second cousin," he said quickly. "There are three of us."

A suspicious look crossed the Tartar's face. "And your name is Yuri, too?"

"Yes," Bolan replied. "With whom do I have the honor of speaking?"

"Vashenko, colonel, GRU. Just thought I'd drop by to welcome you to Cambodia."

"Thank you, comrade," said Bolan.

Vashenko stood up and started toward the door.

Bolan looked around for a weapon. He realized the man knew he wasn't Karkor.

Bolan grabbed his chair and aimed for Vashenko's head. But the man was too quick and parried the blow with a raised arm. The chair broke, and Vashenko crashed into a table that splintered as it cushioned his fall. He was on his feet by the time Bolan had armed himself with another chair. And Vashenko now faced Bolan with one of his own.

They circled each other, Bolan holding his chair straight ahead of him, Vashenko holding his raised like a club. Vashenko was the first to attack. Although he was bigger than Bolan, he moved with deceptive speed. Bolan blocked the blow, knocking Vashenko's weapon out of his hands. The Russian lunged, hands outstretched, going for Bolan's throat. Bolan sidestepped, and the Tartar crashed into a chest of drawers.

The man uttered a string of curses as he came at Bolan again. Bolan dodged the charge, but his heel landed on a piece of broken wood and he fell, hitting his head on the floor. A moment later Vashenko was on top of him, sitting astride his chest, his huge hands around Bolan's throat.

Bolan fought to free himself, punching and twisting. It

was like being trapped under a two-ton truck. He could hit the Tartar as much and as hard as he was able but it was useless. Bolan saw yellow, the first sign of asphyxiation. Frantically his hands began groping the floor for a weapon. His left hand found a piece of table leg. He hit Vashenko in the side, the blow momentarily loosening the man's grip.

They rolled, Bolan up one moment, down the next. Vashenko pinned him and again his hands clasped Bolan's throat. Bolan grabbed one of the Tartar's wrists with both his hands to try a *nikio* in jujitsu. But the man had wrists the size of knee joints. Again Bolan saw yellow, and this time there was no wood handy.

The yellow haze grew in luminosity and black spots appeared. A loud buzzing began sounding in Bolan's ears. This was it. He was going under. Frantically he began rocking in preparation for a final heave but it was too late. His legs and arms weakened, blackness invaded his eyes. The buzzing turned to the rushing of water and he felt himself falling from a great height.

The next thing he knew he had stopped falling. He opened his eyes to see Eng, naked and dripping with water, furiously clubbing Vashenko with another table leg. The Tartar lay unconscious a few feet from Bolan, the side of his head bloody from the sharp edges of the makeshift club.

"Enough!" Bolan shouted. He did not want blood on the floor.

The command brought Eng to her senses and she stopped. For a moment she stood panting over the Tartar, her eyes glazed. Then, realizing she was nude, she dropped the wood and ran into the bedroom.

Bolan stood and approached Vashenko, stepping over

the broken furniture and the papers that were strewn on the floor. He inspected the Tartar. The man was definitely out.

He took the tail end of Vashenko's suit jacket and pulled it under his head so it would absorb the blood. He lifted the Russian and dragged him toward the bathroom.

"What are you going to do?" Eng asked. She had emerged from the bathroom wearing a bathrobe.

"Kill him," Bolan said simply.

He went into the bathroom, took a towel from a rack and tore it into strips. These he knotted together, then tied the ends to the leg. Now he had a garrote.

He returned to Vashenko and turned him over on his stomach, passed the cord around his neck and proceeded to twist the table leg. Bit by bit the cord began to bite into Vashenko's throat.

Bolan placed a foot on Vashenko's back, took a deep breath and turned the leg as far as it would go. Nothing happened. Vashenko had a neck like a bull, his carotid arteries protected by thick muscle.

Again Bolan twisted with all his might. Vashenko's tongue came out, his eyelids opened and his eyeballs bulged. The face turned purple as the noose around Vashenko's neck squeezed the carotids, cutting off the blood to the brain.

Sweat dripped from Bolan's body and his arms were going numb, but still he did not relax the tension on the noose. The Tartar looked grotesque. Bolan looked at the distended pulse at the man's temple. At last the heartbeat was growing fainter.

Finally Bolan let go of the garrote and stepped away. The table leg spun back, clacking on the stone floor. The cord slackened, revealing a deep red-blue welt on Vashenko's neck. Bolan kneeled by his side and felt for his pulse. Nothing.

Vashenko was dead.

Bolan stood, took a towel and wiped himself. His cover was safe once more. But now he had to figure out a cover for Vashenko. He would soon be discovered missing from the wedding reception.

THE HOTEL'S DINING ROOM was noisy with a garrulous crowd trying to make itself heard over the music. A quartet of Cambodian guitarists was playing Moscow Nights, the singer struggling with the Russian words.

They sat at tables—gross, vulgar people, their faces red from liquor, sweaty from the heat and smoke. Bolan viewed them with distaste. It was their kind—those who kowtowed to authority and kissed asses—that kept Communism going in Russia. They were men and women who had sold their souls in return for rubles and the right to travel abroad. And while they lived the good life, other Russians, those who would not toe the party line, who spoke up against injustice, did not squeal on their parents, those unfortunates lived in a giant jail. The more outspoken of them were deported to slave in KGB mines or stew in KGB psychiatric asylums.

Eng looked about the room, then returned her gaze to Bolan.

"What do you think of this crowd?" he asked.

"I think they should return to their land of snow and ice." In a quieter voice she added, "Someone is coming."

"Engineer Patiushek," the man said, introducing himself. "Excuse this interruption, Major Karkor, but have you seen Colonel Vashenko?"

"I did earlier," Bolan said. "He came to see me in my room. We talked for a while, then he left."

"He is not at dinner, he is not in his room and no one has seen him."

Bolan turned to Eng, who mumbled something. Bolan addressed Patiushek in Russian, "My wife says he may have gone into town. He did mention something about buying flowers."

"Flowers?"

"I think he's got a woman in town," Bolan said conspiratorially.

"I see," the engineer said, perplexed. "What should we tell his wife?" He added in an undertone, "She is the lady in the pink dress."

Bolan's eyes swept the room in search of the woman, his mind whirling. If Vashenko's wife knew Karkor. . . .

But she did not. He could tell from her expression as she looked at him. Bolan turned back to Patiushek. "Tell her," he said, "that he was called away on official business. Say he's with the Vietnamese, that he might be late getting back."

The engineer left their table.

"So now we have a wife to worry about," Bolan said. He watched the engineer talk to Vashenko's wife. She seemed none too happy as she glanced in Bolan's direction.

Bolan bowed and the woman responded with a nervous smile.

Eng put her fork down. "When she finds that her husband is not back in the morning, she will call the police."

"No she won't," Bolan said.

"How do you know?" Eng snapped.

"She'll be dead."

WHEN THE RECEPTION WAS OVER, Bolan went to the front desk and asked for the room number of Colonel Vashenko.

A little while later, he climbed to the second floor and walked down the dark corridor. Light came from under many of the doors, including twenty-six, the number the clerk had given him. Bolan knocked and the door was opened almost immediately. Vashenko's wife wore a robe over a nightdress.

"May I come in?" he asked in a grave voice, entering without waiting for an answer.

"Is it about Andrei?" she asked, alarmed.

"Your husband is in my room," he said. "He was involved in a fight. Can you get dressed and come up?"

"Is he hurt?"

Bolan put a finger to her lips. "We don't want a scandal. A few grazes. Please get dressed. By the way, not a word to anyone. I'll be upstairs. Room thirty-four."

He returned to his suite and opened the wall closet of the sitting room where Vashenko's body lay amid broken furniture. He rummaged through the broken wood, picked up a table leg and placed it on an armchair.

The bedroom door was closed. Bolan opened it, glanced in, saw Eng asleep and closed the door. He took off his jacket and covered the table leg on the armchair, then checked the room for any reflective surface that might warn her as he came for her. But the curtains were drawn and there was no mirror. He paused to listen. From the suite next door came the sound of a conversation.

A few minutes later there was a knock on the door. He let her in. "He's in the bedroom," said Bolan quietly.

A look of alarm crossed her face, and she hurried for the door. Bolan followed her. As he passed the armchair, he picked up the table leg and hit her over the head. There was a sharp crack, then a moan as her legs gave way and she crumpled to the floor.

Bolan stood over her, listening. From next door the conversation went on as usual. He pulled the Russian woman to the center of the room and turned her over on her stomach. He bent over and reached for her wrist. Satisfied there was no pulse, he dragged her to the closet and shoved her in next to her dead husband. He turned off the light and went into the bathroom.

He took a shower then crawled under the mosquito net beside Eng. Not once did she stir. She lay atop the covers. He decided to follow her example.

He stretched out, thinking of the day ahead. Tomorrow he would find out if there was a POW camp in Cambodia with Americans in it. Not that he doubted its existence anymore, but experience had taught him not to believe anything until he saw it himself.

Tomorrow he would know if the mission was for real.

He had returned once again to Southeast Asia to fulfill his destiny. The League of Families had contacted him through his friend and ally Hal Brognola, because its members were desperate for help in rescuing their men from an overseas incarceration to which they had been abandoned by their government.

A representative of the LOF knew Brognola personally and had hoped the Fed would assist the organization directly. What that representative did not know was that Hal had a warrior in mind for the job, who urgently needed to get the hell out of the United States for a while.

The warrior was Mack Bolan, the Executioner, whose transformation from counterterrorist John Phoenix to lone vigilante of justice and personal war had captured the attention of the very highest levels of government in Washington, D.C.

Mack Bolan had to keep moving. He needed to increase his chances of staying invisible while moving remorselessly against his enemies on all fronts everywhere. This plea from families who in their sadness and defiant determination echoed the passion of his own family, gave him the perfect opportunity to get out of the firing zone of the domestic front and into—what? The fire?

He hoped so.

4

The fort, a huge white structure that reflected the light of the sun, stood on a promontory jutting out to sea. From the ramparts a red flag with a yellow star rippled in the breeze. At the appearance of the Gaz, the big bronze gates swung open, and Bolan drove into an outer courtyard. A young lieutenant materialized from a side door, mounted the step of the jeep and instructed Bolan to continue.

Bolan and Eng went through several more gates and courtyards before emerging onto a large parade ground. By a central flagpole, flying another yellow star, stood an honor guard. Bolan pulled up in front and they disembarked.

A colonel in a burgundy beret set at a jaunty angle stepped forward and saluted. "Colonel Minh, the camp commandant," the young lieutenant whispered. The honor guard presented arms, and loudspeakers blared a Russian martial tune.

Bolan stood at attention, studying the soldiers. They were a tough-looking lot, mountain troops, veterans of a war that had humiliated the biggest power on earth. Never mind that the power made only a halfhearted effort; they fought like lions and won. Bolan respected them for it.

The colonel saluted as the loudspeakers switched to the Vietnamese national anthem. Minh was considerably older than his men, a father figure with closely cropped hair and a weather-beaten face. On his chest was a solitary green-and-red ribbon, the Order of Dien Bien Phu, the battle in which France lost its empire in Asia.

The anthem over, Bolan inspected the guard. Not a speck of dust anywhere, not a crease out of place. To take on this lot with guerrillas would require at least a ratio of five-to-one....

"How big is your garrison?" Bolan asked. They had come to the end of the line.

"Two hundred eighty men," the colonel replied. "And fifty at the mine."

"Superb troops," Bolan said. He reached into his sleeve as if to adjust his watch and turned on the Sony tape recorder he carried in an inside pocket. "Is it not waste, though, to have them doing prison duty?"

"The mine is a big money-maker for our government," the colonel said. "As you know we own half. An operation of such magnitude is too valuable to be left to prison troops."

"The troops don't mind?"

"For them it is a holiday. We rotate the garrison every two months."

Bad news, Bolan thought. A rotating garrison would be alert.

"And now, I invite you for a *vin d'honneur*," the colonel said.

"Before we go, Colonel, I wonder if my wife could take a picture of us?" Bolan asked. "She is putting together an album of our trip."

The Agfa clicked three times, each shot taken from a different angle, showing a different aspect of the fort. They were not pictures of prisoners, but it was a beginning.

They set out across the parade ground, Bolan's eyes taking in the fort's defenses. They were nothing special—machine guns on the ramparts, mortar on the ground—but nothing special was needed with those walls. They were four stories high and a good two yards thick.

Karkor was right, Bolan realized. To breach the walls would require cannon, which the guerrillas did not have. The only other possibility was to stage an assault over the wall, but for that they would need mortar-fired grappling hooks. The guerrillas did not have those, either.

An inside job, then. That was the only way the fort could be captured. And for that he would need help from the prisoners.

"I don't see any prisoners," he said.

"All are at the mine."

They entered the building and climbed a stone stairway, then made their way along a corridor. On the walls hung watercolors showing scenes from the Vietnam War. They showed both Americans and Vietnamese.

They entered the officers' mess, where the camp staff was assembled. One by one the men were presented to Bolan. All were regular army officers, young men, bright, fully awake. Even an inside job might take some doing, Bolan thought.

A round of toasts was followed by speeches. The colonel spoke of the need for close unity between Vietnam and the USSR to maintain peace in Asia. Bolan, speaking as Karkor, promised that the Soviet Union would maintain its vigilance in the face of U.S. imperialism and Chinese hegemony.

Next came a tour of the actual prison. To Bolan's surprise there were no cells or bars. The prisoners slept in dormitories, the rooms bright and airy, and there was a lot of personal bric-a-brac, always a measure of freedom.

They passed the library, a movie theater, snooker room, Ping-Pong room, gymnasium, a modern cafeteria. There was even a multidenominational chapel.

"Doesn't look like a jail to me," Bolan observed.

"We try to make life as pleasant for them as possible," the colonel said. "After all, they make money for us."

They came to the dormitory housing the Americans. On a wall hung a huge reproduction of a recruiting poster showing Uncle Sam pointing his finger at the viewer. However, instead of the words "I want you," the caption read, "Screw you."

"Do you speak English, Major?"

"Very little," Bolan replied.

The colonel translated. "There is considerable resentment among the men against their governments for not paying the war reparation Vietnam is demanding," he explained. "They feel their countries have abandoned them."

"Which they have," Bolan said. He turned to Eng. "Take a picture, dear. It's rather amusing."

The camera clicked twice. One close-up shot, one long shot, the latter showing bed and plaques with names.

They walked on, passing a washroom. "Would you mind?" Bolan said. He disappeared inside, changed the cassette in his Sony, pulled the chain and came out. "I see no bars," he stated. "The prisoners don't take advantage?"

"We've had only one escape attempt in two years," the colonel said. "A couple of Americans and a South Korean killed a guard and escaped through a side door. But they didn't get far. A fisherman reported them, and they were caught the same day."

"So the locals cooperate," Bolan remarked.

"We have very good relations. The local population realizes we are here to protect them. Are you familiar with what went on under the Khmer Rouge?"

"Yes, I heard."

"It boggles the mind."

"How were the escapees punished?" Bolan asked.

"They were hanged. We have an understanding in this camp: in return for a measure of freedom, escapees are punished by death."

They came out onto a courtyard. A trio of vehicles awaited them: a command car and two jeeps with mounted machine guns. They boarded the command car.

"The mine is only a three-minute drive, but when I have visitors I always take an escort," the colonel said. "The hills are full of bandits."

Bolan nodded. The vehicles set off and soon a turn appeared in the road. The leading gun jeep opened up, spraying the sides in case anyone was hiding in the bushes.

The convoy crested a hill, and the mine came into view. It lay in a sandy bowl, a cluster of buildings around a shaft head-frame and a hoist shed, the lot encircled by a wire fence and miradors. A strip of freshly plowed earth ran at the foot of the fence.

"Is that a mine field?" Bolan asked.

"Double-decker mines," the colonel replied. "Lift one, the other explodes. The fence is electrified, and the miradors are armed with fifty-caliber machine guns. War booty. The Americans left enough to equip several divisions. These mortar emplacements you see are eighty-two millimeter."

"Isn't the garrison rather small for a vital installation?" Bolan asked.

"It's a skeleton for internal security only. In case of external attack we could quickly reinforce. An underground tunnel links the fort with the mine. By tunnel it's even quicker than by road.''

The entrance to the compound was an archway bedecked with flags and slogans, which is the fashion in factories and mines in Communist lands. They drove in and headed for the administration building. On the way they passed some repair shacks. Two men, wearing brown overalls with names and flags on their chests, one Thai, the other Filipino, sat in the shade. Prisoners.

A few yards further on the convoy drove by a work gang laying foundation for a building. The white foreman turned to look at them. Bolan caught sight of Stars and Stripes on his chest. A forklift, driven by a black man, passed. Another American. A white man emerged from the crusher house carrying a bucket. American.

Bolan's flesh tingled. After all these years of rumor and speculation, there it was, surrounded by the jungle hills of Cambodia—a Vietnamese POW camp with Americans in it.

THE CARS DREW UP in front of a house on stilts. A short, wiry man with pince-nez glasses awaited them at the foot of the steps. There was a round of handshakes, then the colonel and the gun jeeps departed. Bolan and Eng followed the man, who had introduced himself as Thuc, the manager, into the house; it contained a nondescript, one-room office.

They took seats at a table. Thuc served lemonade and, after some preliminary chatter about the ruins of Tonle Wat that Major Karkor had visited en route, the meeting began. Thuc started by giving Bolan an earful of what it was like to run a business in a socialist economy.

Bolan listened patiently, waiting for an opening.

"Expanding the operation will not increase production," the manager went on. "We must first have reforms in the system of supply. In fact, I believe that given reforms we could double output without an increase in manpower."

"Really?" Bolan said.

"The work force here is the best I've had, thanks mainly to my American foremen."

"How interesting," Bolan said, switching on the tape recorder. "The Americans are that good, are they?"

"Efficiency with them is almost a religion," Thuc explained. "In this mine the language of work is English. With so many nationalities, we had to have a unified means of communication. English seemed the most appropriate. The machinery is American, the handbooks are in English and the most qualified personnel are American. We even have an American mining engineer. He acts as my right hand."

"How many Americans are there?" Bolan asked.

"Thirty-five. All but five are foremen. They are new arrivals. I attempted to train other nationalities, but none reached the level of competence of the Americans."

"How interesting," Bolan repeated. "I would like to meet some."

"Americans?" the manager questioned.

Bolan was on the verge of saying yes when he caught himself. In a day or two, the Vietnamese police would descend on the mine and interrogate everyone who had anything to do with him. If he talked only to Americans, suspicion would center on them. They would be interrogated, perhaps tortured, the Vietnamese assuming they were in league with the impostor. He would not expose them to torture.

"Americans, Thais, South Koreans," he replied. "A representative cross section."

Thuc rose and went to the telephone. He moved slowly, a tired man worn out by years of frustration. It was at his level that the Communist system was the most frustrating, Bolan reflected. The people above him had it easy—they merely drew up plans, two-year plan, five-year plan, while those below devoted their energies to doing the least possible work. Thuc was caught in the middle.

"Busy," he said putting the phone down. "Will you excuse me? I think it will be faster if I go myself." He left the office.

Eng moved closer to Bolan. "I was thinking. . . ."

He silenced her with a finger on his lips. "Let's go on the balcony."

They went onto the veranda. To their left the crusher house spewed ore, making a racket. The ore bobbed along a conveyor belt on the way to the mill. The sand baked in the sun, the buildings shimmered in the heat. The day was going to be another scorcher. Bolan and Eng stood close together, so they could make themselves heard above the noise.

"I was thinking we should attack the mine instead of the fort," Eng said. "The mine is a much easier target. If we capture it quickly, we could block the tunnel. They could not reinforce. We could block the road, too."

"Wouldn't work," Bolan said. "First it would mean a daylight attack. The prisoners are here only during the day. And there must be a good hundred kilometers of tunnels. We would have to hold the mine for hours, and the enemy would surround us. They'd even have time to bring troops from Yen Sai."

Thuc returned to announce he had found seventeen people. They were assembling by the power station. He suggested Bolan and Eng go there right away.

The seventeen turned out to be a mixture of surface and underground workers, the latter in helmets with lamps and grimy from dirt. Five American foremen were among them, the ones who ran the surface installations.

Bolan spoke to all seventeen. He asked questions in Vietnamese, which the manager translated into English. With everyone he kept to the same format.

"Name, rank, military function?"

"Jim Barnes, captain, United States Air Force."

"How were you captured?"

"I was shot down on a bombing mission over North Vietnam."

"Date?"

"March 1969."

"What do you do at the mine?"

"I am a chemist at the mill."

All the time the Sony recorded.

After he got the basic information from each prisoner, he asked general questions to make his interrogation more natural. Did they know why they were still prisoner? How were they treated? They all replied they were treated properly and all knew why they were still there. They spoke without bitterness in the manner of men resigned to their fate. They had come to accept their slavery and tried to make the best of it.

As he was about to leave, a sixth American showed up. The manager presented him as Major Cosgrove, his right hand man. Bolan permitted himself a variation from the format.

"I have heard very favorable reports about you Americans."

"We try to do our job," Cosgrove said.

"How many Americans are there?"

"Thirty-five."

Bolan now had a confirmation of the figure from an American. He switched off the Sony, and they walked back to the administration building.

"Have you a list of the prisoners?" he asked.

"They are all listed in the workbook," the manager replied.

"I must copy it."

"Don't they have one in Hanoi?"

"This is for the Phnom Penh office."

They entered the office. Thuc gave Bolan the workbook and he proceeded to copy the names. First he copied the American names, then the others. Meanwhile, Eng was keeping the manager busy with talk about his family.

The telephone rang and Thuc answered it. "Yes, he's here," Bolan heard him say. "I beg your pardon?" A long silence followed. Bolan's insides stirred. He could feel sweat break out about his collar. He went on scribbling names.

The receiver went down. "There must be a mistake," the manager said in a hushed voice. "That was the police. They are coming to arrest you. They said I was not to allow you to leave."

Bolan and Eng exchanged glances. The manager lifted the receiver. He was going to call the garrison.

"Put it down," Eng snapped. In her hand gleamed a silver-plated lady's pistol. It had belonged to Madame Karkor.

Thuc looked at Bolan. "You'd better do as she says," Bolan said. "She's a very good shot."

The man replaced the receiver.

Bolan closed the workbook and placed it on Thuc's desk. "Now you have a choice," he instructed. "Either you drive us out of here or we shoot you and drive ourselves."

"Not much choice," the manager said, rising briskly.

It was always interesting to see a man's reaction in the face of danger, Bolan thought. So many times it was surprising, as with this man. Until then he had been somewhat lethargic. Suddenly energy flowed from him.

They went out and got into the Gaz, the manager behind the wheel. A minute later they drove out under the arch with the flags. The guard in one of the miradors waved a greeting. Three minutes later they passed the fort.

"Where are we going?" the manager asked.

"Just keep driving," Bolan told him. "Did the police say when the patrol left?"

"They said it was leaving immediately."

"He could be lying," Eng cautioned. "They could be near here already."

"Why should I lie?" the manager said. "At my age one is not interested in heroics."

"Stop here," Bolan ordered.

Thuc brought the jeep to a halt. "I suppose this is where you shoot me."

"No one is going to shoot you. Step out." Bolan slid behind the wheel. "You have only two kilometers to walk."

"What do I tell the police?" the manager asked.

"Tell them I killed the couple in the hotel out of revenge. Tell them it was an affair between Russians. Goodbye."

He drove off.

"I would have killed him," Eng said.

"What for?" Bolan asked. "Dead he serves no purpose. Alive he will help confuse the police."

The jeep picked up speed.

"You remember the trail we passed?" Eng said. "When we get to it, turn left. It leads to a village. We will borrow ponies. By evening we should be in my village." She brought the Agfa out from her handbag and handed it to Bolan. "I hope P'um is safe. If he has been arrested, I won't come with you to Thailand."

"I understand," Bolan said, putting the Agfa in his pocket.

"When do you want to leave?"

"As soon as you can arrange it." He had all the information the League required—proof of a POW camp, proof that Americans were in it, plus verbal confirmation by Cosgrove that there were thirty-five. And he had their names. Now all he had to do was deliver the information to the League. He was impatient to get going.

"How about tonight?" he asked.

"We'll see," Eng answered.

Suddenly a burst of gunfire hit the air.

The wheel spun out of Bolan's hand and the Gaz left the road.

A tree rushed at them.

Bolan felt the impact, then everything went black.

5

A slap on the face brought Bolan to his senses. He lay in a hut, propped against the wall, hands tied behind his back. The place was gloomy and smelled of dampness from the earthen floor. By his side squatted a slant-eyed midget in a camouflaged uniform and an oversized bush hat. He was doing the slapping.

"Awake, awake, Major Karkor," he jovially called in Vietnamese. He had a high-pitched, almost feminine voice.

"Where am I?" Bolan asked, swallowing hard. He felt groggy and his throat was parched.

"You are prisoner of National Union for an Independent, Neutral, Peaceful and Cooperative Kampuchea." It was the official name for Moulaka. "You want water?" the midget added.

Bolan nodded. "Who are you?"

"Van Ngo," he replied. Then he snapped an order to a Montagnard cradling an Armalite at the door. The guard went to a drum of water, filled a pail and handed it to the midget. As Van Ngo turned to take it, Bolan saw he was armed with a Luger. Like the hat, it looked oversized for him.

"Drink," the man said, pouring the water slowly into Bolan's mouth.

"What time is it?" Bolan asked between sips.

"Five o'clock."

Bolan realized he had been out for nearly six hours.

"You were given chloroform so you sleep during ride," Van Ngo said. "The woman also. She sleeping in another hut."

"Is she all right?" Bolan asked.

"You both not hurt," Van Ngo told him.

"Why did you ambush us?"

The midget grinned, revealing a gold front tooth. "You are prisoner for ransom. You write letter to USSR embassy in Phnom Penh. Embassy send money. We send Major Karkor."

"I am not Major Karkor."

"Ha, ha, you are funny."

"It's true. I am an American agent. I'm the man your side ambushed during the storm."

At the mention of the storm, the midget's face clouded. "What storm?" he asked less jovially.

"There was a storm the day I arrived in Cambodia. I arrived by sea. You ambushed the Khmer Rouge waiting for me on the beach."

"You are very funny." But his eyes belied his cheer.

Three heads passed on the other side of the flap that served as a window. The door opened. An aristocratic-looking individual entered, swagger stick in hand. He wore riding breeches, knee-high boots and a wide-brimmed hat with a tiger-skin band.

The midget jumped to attention. A conversation in Khmer followed during which the visitor kept tapping his boot with the stick. They made a real pair, Bolan observed, the midget and the partisan dandy.

"You're an American?" the visitor asked Bolan. He spoke English with a French accent.

"Yes. My name is Mack Bolan." He repeated what he

had told the midget. "My companion will vouch for me."

"That she-devil is no recommendation," said the visitor. "Whom do you work for?"

"I cannot tell you," Bolan said.

The man studied him in silence, the swagger stick tapping the boot. "Come outside."

Bolan stood and followed him out of the hut. He was in a Montagnard village amid jungle hills. The tribesmen were Saoch; he could tell by the women's costumes.

"Open your mouth," the dandy said. "Go on, open it." He looked inside, twisting Bolan's face this way and that. "You are an American," he said finally. "I can tell by your fillings." He spoke to one of the Montagnards and the man cut Bolan's bonds.

Bolan now knew who the man was—Nordom Parong, one of Prince Sihanouk's forty-three sons. Bolan had read about him. Parong was a dentist who had given up his profession in Thailand to fight against the Vietnamese.

"You're Captain Parong, aren't you?" Bolan said.

"Prince Captain Parong," he corrected him. "And you? What are you doing here? Preparing the ground to rescue POWs?"

"I am not at liberty to tell you."

"I played your cassettes," Parong informed him. "You'd be better off working with us than the Khmer Rouge. We can be trusted, they can't."

Bolan said nothing.

"I will send some food," Parong said. "In the meantime, I will check with my superiors to see what they want to do with you. Van Ngo, take him inside."

The midget led Bolan back into the hut. "Major Karkor an American agent, yes?"

"That's what I told you in the first place," Bolan said.

"I not clever like the chief," Van Ngo said. "The chief very clever man. See." He pointed to his gold tooth. "Tooth belong to Vietnamese colonel. Chief take it and give it to me. Not clever?"

"Very," Bolan said, taking a seat.

The food arrived—some sticky rice, dried fish, prahoc sauce and tea. As Bolan was nearing the end of the meal, Parong brought Bolan's camera and tape recorder.

"Your things," he said. "I am sending you to the main base. They want to talk to you. You'll leave immediately." He turned to the midget and spoke in Khmer.

"I really don't have time to visit your base," Bolan remarked. "I am on my way to Thailand."

"A two-day detour, no more," Parong said. "Our G-2 are interested in why the U.S. government ignored our information on the POW camp and decided to work with the Khmer Rouge."

"I was not sent by the U.S. government," Bolan said.

"Explain that to them," Parong said. He touched the brim of his bush hat with the swagger stick. "A pleasant journey."

"What about my companion?" Bolan asked.

"You can forget about your companion. Captain Macdok is under arrest."

"Under arrest?"

"For murder." Parong left the hut.

"Ha, ha, we go together," said Van Ngo, jovial once more.

Bolan's mind raced. He couldn't abandon Eng. She came here with him; she was going to leave with him.

The problem was how to get her out of here. He was alone. They had fifty, perhaps a hundred guerrillas. As he worked on a plan he saw Van Ngo staring at the tape recorder and the camera. Like all primitive people, he was fascinated by technology. There was the key, Bolan told himself. He put away the Agfa and the Sony, and stood up.

"Okay, let's go," Bolan muttered.

They went outside, and the little man led him to a flame tree beside which crouched two Montagnards who would accompany them. Next to them stood four ponies. The midget left Bolan in their care and went to fetch his haversack and weapon. A crowd of villagers gathered around Bolan.

"American?" asked the elder of the Montagnards.

"Yes."

"We fight for Americans. Long time ago."

"Green Berets?" asked Bolan.

"CIA."

"I fought with the Montagnards in Vietnam," Bolan informed them, taking in the men's weapons. Both Montagnards were armed with Armalites and machetes.

The crowd stirred and there were approving grunts. A long nose who had fought with their kind.

"You look alike," Bolan said.

The elder Montagnard smiled. "I am Thieu and this is my son, Tho." He nodded at the other man.

"Americans come back?" asked a voice in the crowd.

"Perhaps," Bolan said.

"Americans no good," another man spat. "They say fight then leave."

"But they pay well," said a third.

Van Ngo returned, haversack on his back. In his hand he carried a CAR-15.

Bolan and Van Ngo and the two Montagnards mounted the ponies and set off across the village, Bolan keeping an eye for any sign of Eng. There was none.

They climbed a path up the valley slope and turned left on the ridge-top trail. The sun was going down, the sky violet.

Van Ngo rode first, followed by Bolan, Thieu and finally Tho. The elder Montagnard had his gun pointed at Bolan's back. Nothing had been said, but it was clear the midget was not taking any chances. For all his moronic laughter, Bolan suspected he was a shrewd man. But he was a primitive man, and Bolan intended to exploit that to gain freedom.

As soon as they came to a widening in the trail, Bolan turned on the tape recorder and moved to Van Ngo's side. He began a conversation, asking him where he came from, what his family did, why he joined the army. They chatted for about three minutes by which time the path narrowed again and Bolan had to fall back. Bolan rewound the cassette.

At the next widening, Bolan returned to Van Ngo's side.

"This is embarrassing. That damn supper I ate has given me indigestion," Bolan groaned, hoping the man was not familiar with the effect of sticky rice on Westerners. Normally it was the other way around, it caused constipation. "Could we stop for a moment? I need to relieve myself."

Van Ngo gave a suspicious look from under the bush hat.

"Don't worry, I wouldn't be so foolish," Bolan said, reading the man's mind. "All alone in the jungle, and in a Russian uniform? I wouldn't get very far, would I?"

Van Ngo halted. He snapped an order to the Montagnards and everyone dismounted. He motioned for Bolan to lead the way. They went into the trees, the midget's gun pointing at Bolan's back.

"While I go, listen to this," Bolan said, handing Van

Ngo the tape recorder. He pressed the playback key and the midget's voice came on. The man was startled, eyes filled with awe. "Take it." But Van Ngo stepped back as if afraid to touch it.

Bolan put the recorder on the ground and went behind the bushes. He waited for half a minute, then emerged, buttoning up his trousers. Major Karkor's pants did not have a zipper. Van Ngo was crouching by the recorder, listening to his voice. At Bolan's appearance, he grinned sheepishly. Bolan picked up the recorder, stopped it and rewound the cassette. He held it out to the midget.

"Play it."

The midget put the CAR-15 between his legs and took the recorder. Bolan bent over to show him how to hold it in his left hand and use his right index finger to press the playback key. As Van Ngo pressed it, Bolan put his arms around the man's neck in a choke hold.

The recorder fell to the ground and continued to play while the man struggled to free himself, his grunts drowned out by his own voice on tape. Bolan pressed with all his weight. Bit by bit Van Ngo's movements weakened and he went limp. Bolan laid him down, took his dagger and plunged it into his heart.

Bolan picked up the Sony and the CAR-15. He filled his pockets with magazine clips from the ammo pouch. Then, weapon in one hand, tape recorder still playing in the other, he went back to the trail. Only as he stepped out did he switch it off. He did not want to panic the Montagnards with it. They might think the little man had disappeared inside the machine.

"Drop your weapons," Bolan ordered.

The Montagnards stared at the rifle, confusion on their faces. One moment they were listening to Van Ngo's voice, the next the American appeared with his gun. The elder Montagnard was the first to obey, his son followed.

Bolan told them to move to another spot, leaving their guns and machetes behind. When they did, he collected the arms and told them to sit down.

"Van Ngo is dead," he announced. "I am returning to the village to rescue the woman. If you help me I will pay you in gold."

"And what afterward?" Thieu asked. "The chief will kill us."

"You don't need to remain in the village. You will be able to live anywhere you like, because you will be rich. I will pay you twenty gold dollars each. In paper money, that is seven hundred each."

"Seven hundred!" Tho exclaimed. It was more than he would make in a lifetime.

"Seven hundred," Bolan repeated. "I will pay the money when we reach the Khmer Rouge village. I swear on the spirits. May they smite me if I break my word."

"We have families in village," Thieu said.

"Your families can join you."

"The chief will take revenge."

"He won't know you helped me. We will enter the village when everyone is sleeping. You will not be seen."

"Seven hundred dollars," Tho said, looking at his father. It was clear he opted for a change of employers.

"Seven hundred *each*," Bolan said. "But if you agree to help me, you must swear on the spirits that you will be loyal and not cheat me. And if you do cheat me, I will kill you and throw your bodies to the dogs. Without a grave, your souls will wander the world for eternity."

"If we refuse to help you?" Thieu asked.

"I will kill you, like I killed Van Ngo," Bolan said.

There was a long silence. Tho spoke to his father in Saoch.

"Well?" Bolan asked. "What is your decision? Do I kill you or do you work for me?"

Thieu looked at his son, then at Bolan.

"We work for you," he said.

THE STRAW ROOFS of the village huts seemed silvery in the moonlight. Open doorways glowed with indoor fires and somewhere a child was crying. Atop the ridge, Bolan and his two Montagnards waited for the villagers to go to bed. The only people still outside the huts were men sitting around a campfire smoking water pipes, their last smoke before retiring.

"Where are the guards?" Bolan whispered.

"On all the trails," Thieu replied. He pointed to an area halfway down the slope.

Bolan gave Tho his machete.

"Kill the guard with this. No noise."

"To surprise will be difficult," Thieu remarked.

"He doesn't need to surprise," Bolan said. "Go up to the guard," he said to Tho. "Say Van Ngo sent you back. Your pony broke a leg."

"The guard will be suspicious. My son is without his gun."

It could be a trick, Bolan thought. On the other hand, the man had a point. He gave Tho his gun. "Afterward return here. Your father and I will be waiting."

He nodded knowingly. He understood that his father would be held hostage. "I will come back."

"Wait." Bolan realized that Tho could tell the guard to tip off the village and return claiming he had killed him. "Bring back his ears."

They watched him go.

"You don't trust us?" Thieu asked.

"If I didn't trust you I would have taken the ammunition from your son's gun," Bolan said.

The village darkened momentarily as a cloud covered the moon, then the settlement lit up again. From the houses came various sounds. In one a woman was shouting and a dog was yelping; in another pots and pans clattered, but the smokers were breaking up. There were loud good-nights.

"Where are they keeping the woman?" Bolan asked.

"We don't know," Thieu said. "But I will ask my wife. If she doesn't know she will find out."

Bolan nodded.

A cloud blotted out the moon again. "Come," said Bolan, rising. He led the elder tribesman to another spot— just in case Tho decided to ambush him.

"Why we move?" Thieu asked.

"Your son could be captured," Bolan explained. "The guard could force him to show where we are."

Bolan listened, but heard nothing. From his days with the Montagnard, Bolan knew they had a highly developed sense of hearing.

A little later a twig snapped, marking the approach of Tho. Not seeing them, he began calling to his father in Saoch, *"Mede!"*

"Over here," Bolan said.

Tho appeared with a second Armalite over his back. He held out his hand, palm open. Two lumps. Bolan took the still-warm ears, sticky from blood, and put them in his pocket. To throw them away would be bad manners.

"Who was it?" Thieu asked.

"One of Sa To's sons," the younger Montagnard replied.

"No loss," replied Thieu.

"We go?" Tho asked Bolan.

"A moment," Bolan answered. He took the other Armalite from his back and gave it back to the father.

"You trust us," said the elder Montagnard, pleased.

"I trust you," Bolan said. He had nothing to worry about anymore. By killing one of their own, both men were compromised.

They set off down the trail, leaving the ponies tied to trees. They passed the place where the guard had been killed and turned off onto another path. This one skirted the village. They came to a spot where the track ran nearest to Thieu's house. When they stopped Thieu glanced up to make sure he had plenty of cloud cover, then he broke into a run.

Bolan and Tho waited, Bolan studying the village. By now the doorways were closed for the night. He could see flickering fires through cracks in the walls. They would be kept going all night, providing warmth.

After some minutes Thieu reappeared, running crouched over toward them. "The Khmer Rouge woman is in the shaman's house," he announced, panting. "It's on the other side of the village and there are two guards. We continue."

They moved along the trail. In the village the only creatures now up were dogs and pigs wandering between the houses in the moonlight. The dogs ignored them. Although Bolan's scent was foreign, it was mixed with a scent they knew.

They came to the other side of the village and crouched. Thieu pointed to the back of a house next to a banana tree. The shaman's house.

They agreed on a plan. Bolan scooped some earth,

mixed it with saliva and smeared it on his face and arms.

A cloud hid the moon. "Now."

Bent over, feet moving quietly in the sandy earth, they ran to the rear of the shaman's house and dropped to the ground. A puppy sidled up to Bolan, tail wagging. Bolan caressed it, looking about him, listening.

From the front of the house came a grunt. The guards were there. Bolan took a final look around, then nodded to the Montagnards. They rose and fanned away, each going around to the front from a different side. One would engage in conversation, the other would attack.

"Hey." Bolan heard Thieu grunt a greeting.

"Hey," replied a guard.

A few words were exchanged in an undertone, then there was the swish of machetes and gasps. Bolan rose and ran. As he turned the corner, he saw his men pushing the tips of their machetes into the guards' hearts. He shouldered his gun and lifted the door to prevent scraping.

By the light of a dying fire, he saw two figures on mats. On his left was Eng, curled up under a blanket in her *ao dai*, sandals by her side. To the right, half raised, was the shaman, in her forties with an intelligent, almost good-looking face that spelled danger.

Bolan brought up his weapon. "One word and you're dead." He spoke in Vietnamese, which the Montagnards said she understood.

Behind him, the two Montagnards dragged in the bodies, then the weapons. They went back outside, closing the door behind them. They would remain outside, pretending to be the guards.

The woman kept staring at Bolan, her face partly lit by the fire. Her hair was down. There was something masculine about her.

Bolan went up and pressed the muzzle of his gun against her flat chest. "Lie down," he said. The woman slowly lowered herself, eyes studying Bolan. He could tell she was not in the least afraid.

Bolan turned his head to Eng and called her name in a loud whisper. But Eng went on sleeping. "Eng!" he said again. No good. "Why is she not answering?" he asked the shaman.

"The prince gave her medicine to make her sleep," the shaman replied. Her voice had a manly rasp.

"Turn over on your stomach," Bolan said.

The shaman turned but instead of stopping on her stomach, she rolled all the way around and the next thing Bolan knew she was rising toward him with a knife. The move was so fast he barely had time to block the knife's thrust with his arm. The flashing blade nicked him, making him wince.

They fell to the floor. She fought like a tigress, biting, clawing, using her knee to hit him in the groin, and all the time trying to knife him. It was like fighting three people at once.

The woman's strength and aggressiveness surprised him, but it was this that cost her her life. Once he got over the initial surprise, he realized she was beaten. First he disarmed her with a *sankio* wrist twist, then he rolled atop her and his hands closed around her neck. Her nails sought his eyes, but he kept them out of her reach and all she could do was to scratch his neck and chest. Gradually the oxygen was cut off. She tried clawing at his hands in an effort to free her neck, but it was too late. First one hand, then the other fell away. Her body relaxed and she was dead.

Bolan stood up and went to Eng. He strapped on her sandals and lifted her on to his shoulder. She moaned but went on sleeping. He picked up his CAR-15, opened the door and stepped outside. The Montagnards squatted in the shadow of the house. Following his orders, they had not budged despite the fighting. Bolan looked up, the moon was hidden.

"Let's go!"

They ran for the cover of the jungle. When they got to the trail, he stopped. It was time to consider the Montagnards.

"What did you tell your wife?" he asked Thieu.

"We will send for them. Is the shaman dead?"

"Yes, I had to kill her," Bolan replied. "She attacked me with a knife."

"The village will be sad," Thieu said. "She kept the evil spirits away."

"It was me or her," Bolan said.

A half hour later they were back where they had left the ponies. They put Eng atop Van Ngo's animal and tied her down with lianas.

"Which way?" Thieu asked.

"The coastal road," Bolan instructed, and they rode off.

A STORM CAUGHT THEM EN ROUTE, beating down with such fury that progress was impossible. They rode off the trail and found a huge cave, big enough for men and ponies. The Montagnards lit a fire and settled down for the night, Eng still sleeping. Only Bolan remained awake, his thoughts on the action ahead.

He hoped he was not making a mistake. His plan was to commandeer a vehicle and drive or have themselves driven to the vicinity of Eng's village. From there it was only three hours by foot, so that with luck they could be at the village by nightfall.

The scheme was loaded with risk. There might be road patrols or roadblocks. Yet Bolan could think of no alternate plan. By inland trails it would take three days to reach the village, not counting any unforeseen mishaps like a downed suspension bridge, which would necessitate detours.

Bolan did not have three days. He was in a hurry to communicate the information on the POWs to the League of Families before it became useless.

The longer Bolan delayed, the more time the Vietnamese would have to take preventive steps. Already, he suspected, messages were flying between Yen Sai, Phnom Penh and Hanoi on the subject of the false Major Karkor.

Sooner or later someone would suggest reinforcing the garrison at the fort, or even worse, moving the prisoners to another part of Indochina. They were, after all, worth fifty billion dollars. Less valuable people could be found to work the mine. Neither Hanoi nor the KGB were short of slaves.

Bolan glanced at his watch. It was a little after three in the morning. He must get some sleep, he thought. In a few hours he would need all his wits. He closed his eyes and, lulled by the rain and the thunder, fell asleep immediately.

6

The truck skidded to a halt before a pony tied to a bush on the road. A pith helmet leaned out a window of the cab. Eyes full of fear and suspicion swept the hillside. The face withdrew and there was a muted conversation inside. The occupants of the vehicle, seeing the lone animal, suspected a trap. The cab doors opened and three Vietnamese soldiers emerged, weapons in hand. They pointed the guns at the surrounding jungle, scanning the flora. One of them called out and three more soldiers emerged from under the tarpaulin at the back.

On the side of the hill, hidden by the flora, Bolan and Eng exchanged glances. Bolan was right. Eng had wanted a straightforward holdup to avoid shooting, fearing the noise might give them away to another vehicle. But Bolan preferred to know his enemy's strength before he moved, noise or no noise. Had they staged the ambush as Eng had wanted, the trio in the back of the truck could have shot them.

The soldiers below edged their way to the horse standing on the road near the bush. Such bushes usually signified that the road had been mined in a hurry. When guerrillas had time they hid the mine by burying it.

"Now," Eng whispered.

"Wait," Bolan countered. "One more to come."

Five soldiers stood slightly away from the bush, the sixth

was still by the cab. Bolan decided there was no point in opening fire when one was still by the truck. A bullet in the engine and they were back to square one.

The five men went about inspecting the bush without touching it. Bolan could guess what was going through their minds. It may not be a mine. It may be a booby-trapped bush; the guerrillas also laid those. Or it could be both. No one wanted to be the first to find out.

Finally the sixth soldier joined the others. Bolan lifted his CAR-15 and fired a round. Eng followed suit with the Armalite. At the first report the pony broke its tether and bolted. An instant later the Montagnards opened up from their position behind another bush. Geysers of dirt rose from the road, screams hit the air as men toppled to the ground.

When the firing ceased, five corpses were sprawled on the blood-spattered sand, and a sixth man was crawling for the safety of the jungle. A short burst of gunfire from Bolan halted the escape and brought everything to silence. Bolan listened for the sound of vehicles in the distance. None.

"Go!"

They ran down the hill and boarded the truck, Bolan and Eng hopping into the cab, the Montagnards in the back. Bolan pressed the ignition button. The truck was a Czech Tatra. The engine turned but would not fire. Bolan tried again, the same. He pumped the accelerator and tried once more. Still nothing. Beads of perspiration glistened on his forehead. That's all they needed, a stalled engine. He tried again.

Suddenly an armored car rounded a bend ahead, an eight-wheel Zil going full speed, the Vietnamese flag fluttering from its antenna. The car screeched to a halt at the sight of the corpses on the road.

Bolan grabbed Eng's hand and pulled her out of the cab, ears registering the hum of the Zil's turret as it swiveled the cannon on target. They ran off the road as the car's machine gun opened fire. Bullets thudded into tree trunks and Eng cried out in pain and stumbled. An instant later Bolan, too, was forced down by a blast from the exploding truck.

They hugged the ground, Bolan's arm around Eng. Trees swayed from the explosion and debris rained. A charred leg fell through the canopy.

Goodbye Montagnards.

The machine gun continued firing, the bullets tearing up leaves and branches, eating up the jungle all around them.

Bolan left Eng and crawled back to a tree by the roadway. He waited for a pause in the shooting, then broke cover and came around, his CAR-15 spitting flame. He aimed for the gunner sitting in the turret behind the machine gun. He saw the bullets ricochet off the armor plating. He was firing too low. He was about to let go another volley, higher this time, when the commander disappeared inside.

Bolan ran back to Eng, lifted her and scampered up the hill. A loud bang traveled from the road and a shell swished through the trees. The armored car was going after them with a cannon. Up the hill, the undergrowth flashed orange. Bolan changed direction. Another bang, and another shell came after him.

Pursued by the blistering cannonfire, the hillside reverberating with explosions, Bolan zigzagged through the trees. He was difficult to hit, though the zigzag slowed his progress. Eventually they reached the top and disappeared from view.

"Are you all right?" he shouted as he slid down the other side of the hill.

"Yes," she shouted back.

They crossed a dip, went up another hill and came to a clearing where they had left the other ponies. As he helped Eng onto her mount, Bolan noticed that her leg was bleeding from a thigh wound. He'd attend to it later. He mounted his animal and they galloped off along the ridge-top trail.

Half a mile farther they found a clearing and dismounted, Eng still holding on to her Armalite.

The wound turned out to be a graze, but a bloody one. He took off his shirt, tore it into strips and bandaged Eng's leg.

The job done, he lit a cigarette.

"Okay, the road is out," he said. "What next?"

"We could try the sea," she suggested. "There's a fishing village not far. We might be able to borrow a boat."

"Okay, let's try it."

"We'll have to cross the road."

They crossed a couple of miles from the scene of the ambush. Bolan obliterated the tracks on the road with a branch as best he could.

They rode cross-country and, after an hour, came to the ridge overlooking the sea.

They turned left on a trail, going south. On his right Bolan could see the vast expanse of water shimmering in the sunlight. An oil tanker sailed on the horizon.

The sound of laughter came from up the trail. Bolan and Eng rode into the trees, tied the ponies and moved back to observe the path.

Their fellow travelers turned out to be a couple of peasant women.

"I'm going to talk to them," Eng announced.

Bolan watched her hobble off, supporting herself on the

Armalite. He heard Eng call, and saw the two women stop and retrace their steps. After a long conversation in Khmer, the women continued on their way and Eng returned.

"The Vietnamese have posted a reward for us," she said. "Two men and a woman are wanted for the murder of a Russian official and his wife. One of the men is white, the other Oriental. That means P'um must have got away."

"What's the situation in the fishing village?"

"They're not from that village. But we must watch out. The reward is for twenty thousand riels each. That is what a laborer earns in twenty years. A tempting sum."

They remounted and rode on.

It was a little past noon when they reached the ridge over the village. The settlement was a conglomeration of white-washed houses and huts on stilts bordering a small bay. In the harbor bobbed a few sampans, but that was not what held their attention. A Vietnamese patrol boat was moored to a dock.

"Probably searching for us," Bolan said.

"No, I think they've come for lunch." Eng smiled. "Look."

On a terraced restaurant at the back of what appeared to be a hotel, a group of men in green uniforms and blue sailor hats were being served. He counted eight sailors. That would be about right for the boat. It was a Soviet hydrofoil of the Pchela class, used by the KGB for coastal patrols, or had been until recently, when the KGB got a new model and began selling off the Pchelas to fraternal underdeveloped allies. The boat below was armed with 23mm cannons, one in the bow, one astern.

"The crew could remain in the village for hours," Eng said. "After the meal there will be girls. That hotel is a brothel. One day I will burn it."

Bolan's eyes swept the sampans. "Would any of those have engines?"

"The fishermen can't afford engines. Gasoline is too expensive."

"How long to reach your village by sail?"

"Two days."

Great! Two days to the village to pick up clothes and money, another day to get back to the coast and find a trawler—if they were lucky—and three days to get to Bangkok. Almost a week before he could phone Washington to tip off the League. And another week before a rescue operation could be mounted. Damn. At this rate the fort would be empty before the rescue could begin.

Bolan slid off his pony and walked to the edge of the woods. He lit a cigarette and his nerves gradually calmed, but the impatience remained. There had to be a faster way.

"We commandeer the boat," he said suddenly.

"The gunboat?" Eng's eyes widened.

"Yeah. And instead of going to your village we head directly for Bangkok. That's a hydrofoil down there. It can do close to sixty knots."

"But they are eight," said Eng with a nod at the hotel below. "And we are two."

"That makes the odds even," Bolan said.

ASTRIDE THEIR PONIES the two warriors trotted along the beach in the shade of palms, heading for the hotel. The sun was at its zenith, the sea calm. From the steps of their huts, villagers on their siesta hour watched the newcomers with a guarded air. The white man wore a torn uniform, no shirt and the woman had on a dirty *ao dai*. They rode with reins in one hand, guns in the other. They resembled bandits.

The pair ignored the villagers, eyes riveted on the hotel.

The fishermen were of no consequence—years of war had trained them to wait and see who won before taking sides. The danger came from the hotel. At that distance Bolan and Eng were particularly vulnerable, close enough to be seen but not near enough to attack if someone raised the alarm.

As they neared the brothel, Bolan and Eng heard loud music coming from the upstairs floor. The fun had begun and they had timed it right. Bolan's plan hinged on catching the hydrofoil crew with their pants down.

The boat was on their right, lolling in the water at its moorings. It looked like nothing special, eighty feet of wood and steel painted a dull gray. But inside, Bolan knew, were engines capable of generating six-thousand brake horsepower, and hidden underwater were skids. The combination made hydrofoils one of the fastest craft in existence.

They pulled up by the front door and dismounted, their arrival drowned by the blaring music on the radio. It was rock music, indicating the set was tuned to a station in Thailand—forbidden fruit to the locals for whom listening to foreign radio was punishable by jail.

Guns at the ready, they entered the foyer.

At a table with a checkered cloth sat a middle-aged woman, a bottle of cognac in front of her, and an adding machine and a ledger. She wore jeans and a jacket. The overpainted face hinted that once she had been good- looking.

Her eyes traveled from Eng to Bolan and back to Eng. "Found yourself a stallion, have you?" she remarked snidely. She was drunk.

Eng walked up to her and hit her across the mouth. "Watch your tongue, old hag."

"Why, you!" The woman rose to strike back.

Bolan stepped between them. "Sit down," he said, pushing the brothel keeper back into her chair.

"An American no less," the woman complimented Eng sarcastically. She turned to Bolan. "Come to refight the war?"

"Where are the Vietnamese soldiers?" Bolan demanded.

The woman jerked her head upstairs. "Can't you hear?"

"Are they all up there?" Bolan asked.

"As far as I know," she said, eyes on Eng. The hate that flowed between them was palpable.

"Which room is the captain in?"

"You snake," the woman shouted, ignoring Bolan and going for Eng.

Bolan gave her a clout that sent her back into her chair.

"That bitch killed my husband," the woman spat at Bolan. "My husband who fought for you Americans. And now you Americans are friends with her."

"The world changes," Bolan said.

The woman began to cry. "Why do you come back?" she sobbed. "One war not enough for you?"

"Shoot her and let's get on with it," Eng said. She hobbled to a raffia armchair and returned with a pillow. "This will muffle the shot."

The woman abruptly ceased sobbing. Eyes wide with fear, she looked at Bolan and said quickly. "The captain is in room number six."

"Watch her," Bolan barked at Eng as he headed for the stairs.

The hotel had only two floors. The upper story was essentially a narrow dark corridor with doors leading off either side. There was enough light from under the doors to read the numbers. The radio stood on a table at the end of the hallway.

Bolan tiptoed along the sagging floor. The air smelled of stale sex. From behind the rooms came sounds that the music was supposed to camouflage. He could hear giggles and moans, sagging springs and slapping bodies.

As he reached number six the music stopped. A Thai announcer began reading the day's market prices for pigs and chickens and oxen. The weather forecast followed. Bolan waited until the music resumed, then entered the room.

So engrossed were its occupants they did not even hear him. The captain lay on his back groaning, head turning from side to side. The woman sat astride him, her head thrown back, pumping. Both had their eyes closed.

Suddenly the captain opened his eyes. A look of terror appeared on his face, but he made no move. The sight of Bolan had paralyzed him.

"What's wrong, darling?" the woman asked, opening her eyes.

A startled cry escaped her lips. She crossed her arms to cover her breasts.

Bolan placed a finger on his lips and edged to a chair where the couple's clothes lay. He threw the woman her skirt and blouse and the captain his trousers. In a corner stood the captain's AKM. Bolan shouldered it and waited, listening for any suspicious sound.

Everything was going normally, the radio blaring rock, the couples copulating.

Once the pair had dressed, Bolan stepped into the corridor and motioned for them to come out. They headed downstairs, the woman leading, Bolan following the captain, his gun placed firmly against his back.

In the foyer, the brothel keeper sipped on her cognac, bloodshot eyes staring at the bar till where Eng was counting money. The Khmer Rouge always counted what they stole so they could give a correct receipt.

"We have dollars," Eng announced.

"Okay, let's go," Bolan told Eng. He pushed the captain toward the door. "We're borrowing your boat. You're going to drive."

"I don't have the ignition key," he replied.

Bolan turned him against a wall and searched him. He was telling the truth.

"Who has the key?"

"The chief engineer."

"What's his room number?"

"I don't know."

"He's lying," Eng said. "They come here twice a week, each takes the same woman and every woman has the same room."

"Room number four," said the brothel keeper, resignation in her voice.

Then trouble struck.

A stair squeaked. Bolan looked up and saw a young woman descending. Behind her, a Vietnamese soldier was raising a rifle. Bolan and the captain dived for the floor. Bolan was unable to shoot without hitting the woman. But Eng had no such feelings.

Before the soldier had time to pull the trigger, the Armalite filled the foyer with its roar. The young woman screamed, blood gushing from her stomach. The soldier fell back, face riddled by bullets. Both tumbled down.

Bolan raced for the upper floor. There was a commotion, men shouting, women screaming, doors banging. And all the time the radio played rock. A naked man appeared on the landing, rifle in hand. Bolan fired at point-blank range. The man did a pirouette and tumbled down the stairs past him.

Bolan ran to number four, kicked the door open and stepped aside, waiting for the chief engineer to fire. Instead, a woman screamed. He stepped in to see a naked prostitute backed against a wall, covering herself with a dress. There was no sign of the engineer. A second later he noticed the torn curtain. He went to the window and saw the man hobbling toward the boat. He must have hurt himself leaping. Bolan fired twice and the man went down.

Once again the woman screamed. Bolan ducked and swiveled as hot lead shattered the windowpanes above him. Bolan returned fire and the soldier in the doorway fell back as a round of gunfire stitched a line across his stomach. Downstairs, over the blare of the radio, Eng's Armalite continued chattering.

Bolan risked a look into the corridor. Empty. He strode to the landing. A new corpse had joined the bodies on the stairs. At the foot of the stairs stood Eng, gun ready, the captain cowering at her feet.

"How many did you get?" Eng called up.

"Three," Bolan grunted. "The chief engineer is lying outside."

A door opened in the corridor, then closed quickly. A heavy object came rolling along the floor. There was no room to dive and no point in running. Bolan did the only thing he could do—he kicked it back and stepped aside.

Wham! The building shook and a cloud of dust and cordite blasted out the corridor. The music ceased and in its place rose high-pitched female screams. A trio of women ran out, their clothes in tatters and spattered with blood.

One woman slipped on a blood-soaked stair and all three tumbled down.

The air was heavy with the smell of smoke. Bolan could hear the crackling of flames. A door burst open, feet thudded, a gun opened fire. Bolan went down a few steps. A soldier appeared on the run, shooting from the hip. A short burst by Bolan brought the charge to a halt. The man slid down the stairs and came to rest at Bolan's feet, blood jetting from the neck as his lifeblood drained away.

"I surrender!" a voice shouted from inside the corridor.

A soldier appeared, hands over his head. Bolan ran down the stairs ahead of him to let him descend. Then he signaled to Eng and went out of the hotel and faced the door. Smoke wafted from the upper windows. The ponies, frightened by the shooting, had disappeared.

The captain and the soldier emerged, hands high over their heads. Bolan took over the job of covering the captain, while Eng hobbled by his side. Watched by the villagers, they set out for the wharf. The guarded looks gave way to curiosity—curiosity for this couple who took on eight Vietnamese and won.

They reached the engineer's body, and Eng retrieved the ignition key. The brothel keeper staggered out of the burning hotel and began cursing them. Eng fired a burst and the woman ran back inside. The procession resumed.

"Is it true you killed her husband?" Bolan asked.

"Yes."

"Why?"

"It is of no importance."

They came to the wharf and boarded the hydrofoil. The captain started the engine, the soldier reeled in the mooring ropes and jumped back on the wharf as Bolan had instructed.

"Shoot him," Eng said.

"No."

"He'll run to the road and find a vehicle with a radio. The Vietnamese will send helicopter gunships after us."

She raised her Armalite and mowed the man down in one burst.

Bolan swung the CAR around to face the captain.

"Get going," he commanded.

The terrified captain backed up the hydrofoil and executed a 180-degree turn. He opened the throttle and the engine's rumble grew into a roar.

The boat picked up speed and rose, revealing skids.

Spray flying, they skimmed out of the harbor for the open sea.

7

The hydrofoil skimmed the waves, windshield wipers flapping rhythmically. The wind had picked up and the sea became choppy. From inside the wheelhouse, Bolan observed the gray band stretching across the horizon. They were approaching Thailand. He stood leaning against a wall, gun pointing at the captain's gut. Twice the man had tried to jump them, the first time when showing them how to drive the hydrofoil, the second when Bolan was out lowering the Vietnamese flag and Eng was guarding him. If he tried it again, Bolan intended to shoot him. Both he and Eng now knew enough to control the boat. The only reason they were keeping him was in case of a breakdown.

"We're in Thai waters," the captain announced.

"I know," Bolan said and continued smoking his cigarette.

"Where do you want to get off?"

"Maribou Beach."

"Where is that? I don't know it," whined the captain.

"Fifty kilometers southwest of Bangkok. You can change course now. Take her ten degrees to port."

The hydrofoil banked slightly as the captain turned the wheel. "Is there a harbor?"

"We'll land on the beach."

"The boat will run aground," the captain said. "How will I get back?"

"In two hours' time the second high tide will come in," Bolan told him. He stubbed out his cigarette. "You'll be afloat again."

"Look!" said Eng, pointing in the distance. At eleven o'clock, a circle of spray was advancing toward them. "What is it?"

"A hovercraft," Bolan said, eyeballing the approaching craft.

The captain peered through binoculars, one hand on the steering wheel. "Thai coast guard."

"What is a hovercraft?" Eng asked.

"A boat that travels on a cushion of air," Bolan said.

He took the binoculars and inspected the craft. It was a British-made Winchester. He could tell by the two pylon-mounted propellers at the back. He checked out the artillery. A 20mm cannon was mounted on the front deck and machine guns on the side decks. The cockpit was protected by armor plating.

"He's signaling," Eng said.

Bolan zeroed in on the Morse lamp. "They want us to heave to." He lowered the glasses. "Reduce speed but maintain course," he instructed the captain. He saw Eng look at him with alarm, and he calmed her with a motion of the hand.

The hydrofoil slowed down.

"It's very fast," Eng noted, watching the hovercraft approach.

"A hovercraft is faster than a hydrofoil," the captain said.

"But they have no traction," Bolan told Eng. "And they don't have the maneuverability of a hydrofoil, nor the acceleration." He looked at the captain. "Get ready to accelerate."

"We are not stopping?"

"Only pretending."

"But they will shoot."

"Do as I say," Bolan warned. He returned the glasses to the captain.

The distance between the two boats shrank rapidly.

"I should slow down more," the captain said, "or they'll get suspicious."

Bolan nodded.

The captain cut his speed further, and the boat settled in the water. The ride got bumpier, the hull buffeted by the waves.

The hovercraft also slowed down. Sailors appeared on deck, some holding grappling hooks, others weapons. But those with guns did not give the impression they expected to use them, nor was anyone manning the cannon and the machine guns.

"They must think I am seeking asylum," the captain said.

When the boats got to within forty yards of each other Bolan yelled, "Accelerate!"

The captain's hand reached for the throttle, but instead of opening it he closed it even more.

"Accelerate or I shoot."

The man hurled a black shape at Bolan. He ducked as the binoculars thudded against the wall. In the same instant, Eng's Armalite spat fire and the dead captain flew against the controls.

Bolan grabbed the wheel. He spun it to the right and opened the throttle just as a hook clanged against the side. The hydrofoil shot forward. The Thai sailor holding the hook toppled into the water. Bolan gunned the engine and spun the wheel to the left. The bow of the boat rose as they gained speed and seconds later they were churning up a spray.

"They're coming after us," Eng shouted.

"I'll hold them off with the stern cannon," Bolan said. "Take over." Eng took the wheel as he turned on the intercom so he could communicate while at the gun.

"Look!" Eng cried. Another circle of spray rushed toward them, this one dead ahead.

Bolan had only seconds to think. Run or fight?

"Okay, here's what we do," he said to Eng. He told her his plan. "Just don't lose your nerve."

He ran to the cannon on the foredeck, put on the gunner's helmet and tested the intercom with her. He armed the cannon and aimed it at the approaching boat, waiting.

"And if he does not turn?" Eng's voice said over the earphones.

"He'll turn, don't worry," Bolan replied into his side mike.

He knew the hovercraft by necessity would be the first to turn. Without traction, it required a much bigger radius to change course. The hydrofoil could delay changing direction until the last moment, the hovercraft could not. Bolan intended to exploit that weakness.

The boats converged on each other at a combined speed of more than a hundred knots. The Thais were the first to open fire. Three lines of tracers were directed at Bolan, green from the cannon, flanked by red from the machine guns. Bolan squeezed the trigger of his 23mm weapon. The feeding mechanism rattled, the gun growled and a fourth line of tracers sped over the water—this one yellow.

The boats approached on a collision course, colored projectiles whizzing in both directions. Bolan's eyes were fixed on the hovercraft's pylon-mounted propellers, watching for the tip-off that would tell him which way to swing the gun.

"We're going to crash," Eng's voice said in the earphone.

"No, we won't."

Now. The propellers rotated. The hovercraft would pass on his right.

Immediately he swung the gun and squeezed the trigger. The other craft passed him in a blur, and there were flashes as his rounds exploded in the vessel's side, unprotected by armor. But the hovercraft kept going. Then he spotted another hovercraft skimming the waves toward them.

A loud explosion traveled over the sea. Bolan glanced at the wheelhouse. Eng was shouting to him from behind the window. A pall of smoke in the sky and debris in the water was all there was left of the hovercraft that had passed them.

Bolan ran to the wheelhouse for a better view. The second hovercraft was hot on their tail, but they were approaching the beach. He pointed to a spot where Eng should land, then he raced to find the rope ladder. He carried it to the bow, secured it to the railing and let it fall over the side.

He made his way to the rear cannon. He put on the headset with an earphone and mike—this one did not have a helmet—armed the cannon and opened fire. They were still too far apart for him to hit the hovercraft except by fluke—the choppy water made aim difficult—but there was no harm in trying. He had plenty of ammunition: four belts lay in boxes on deck.

To Bolan's surprise, the hovercraft slowed down. He tried to outguess the pursuer. The tactic could mean two things: the sinking of the other hovercraft had given this one cold feet, or they'd called for helicopters and were merely shadowing him.

"We are coming to land," Eng's voice crackled in the earphone.

The pitch of the engine changed as she cut the throttle; the hull sank. Slowly they rumbled toward the shore. The hovercraft also slowed down to maintain the same distance between them.

"Hold tight," Eng's voice instructed.

The hydrofoil scraped bottom, and she cut the engine. Now Bolan could hear the waves washing over the beach. The keel scraped bottom a second time; the boat shuddered. A third scrape followed. The hydrofoil jolted to a halt and tilted. They were in knee-deep water.

"Now jump off and run," he shouted to her as he resumed firing. At sea the hovercraft was picking up speed, heading for the beach. One of his rounds hit the cockpit and ricocheted into the sky. The armor plating of the cockpit made the boat difficult to damage.

Bolan depressed the cannon and aimed for the boat's black rubber skirt. A round exploded against it. The boat came to a stop and reversed. From the beach came a shot, Eng's signal for Bolan to follow. He had sent her ahead so he could cover her while she limped.

Bolan ran to the ladder and dropped into the water. From the sea he heard a high-pitched whine, and the hovercraft lurched forward full blast. Bolan ran, feet sloshing through the water. There was a good two hundred meters of water to shore at this low tide. Ahead, Eng was on the beach hobbling toward the palms.

Bolan emerged from the sea and sprinted across the sand. There was also a good two hundred meters of sand. A line of tracers whistled past him, the projectiles exploding in the sand ahead. He could hear the cannon fire over the roar of the propellers as the boat bore down. More tracers flew as the machine guns joined in.

Eng reached the palms and began firing her Armalite at the hovercraft. He shouted for her to run, but was drowned out by the noise from the sea.

Bolan glanced behind. The hovercraft was coming out of the water, its black rubber skirt gobbling up land as it advanced. The spray of water gave way to flying sand and driftwood. All three guns were firing. Bolan could hear the whizzing of the projectiles as they flew around him.

The next moment he was inside the thicket of palms. He grabbed Eng's hand and they ran, swerving between the trees, heading inland. Rounds burst everywhere around them, thudding into trunks, ricocheting, tearing up branches and fronds, sending bark flying.

"I can't," Eng cried, stumbling.

Bolan hoisted her in a fireman's carry. He turned and glanced toward the beach. The hovercraft trembled by the tree line, whining like a frustrated animal unable to go any farther. Sailors with guns were jumping to the ground. Bolan fled, carrying Eng.

He went through the undergrowth like a hunted animal, unaware of the razor-sharp thorns and the branches, aware only that he must get deep inside the woods so he could lose his pursuers.

But the forest shelter ended as quickly as it began. Before him was a highway. A car was coming, a big white Buick. Bolan dropped Eng, brought up his weapon and stepped onto the roadway ready to shoot if necessary. This was their last chance.

The car slowed to a halt. A man leaned out. He wore a baseball cap with a Rotary Club badge and a Hawaiian shirt. Before he could open his mouth, Bolan and Eng piled into the back, guns and all.

"Go!" Bolan shouted.

The car sped off, the occupants not saying a word. Two boys, squeezed with Bolan and Eng in the back seat, eyed them with unabashed curiosity. In the front seat a peroxide blonde was looking at her husband with alarm. The husband was looking in the rearview mirror.

"We're going to Bangkok," the man said.

"Good," Bolan said. "We're going there, too." He glanced behind him. Soldiers were emerging from the woods and running across the road into the next field.

"We're from Kansas," the man said.

"We're local," Bolan replied. He glanced at Eng and a look of triumph passed between them. They had made it.

8

Bangkok glowed in the night, its wet streets reflecting the neon lights. On the canals, water taxis sped back and forth past floodlit pagodas. The purr of their engines blended with dance music from an open-air night club. From the tenth floor of his hotel, Bolan observed the sights and sounds of the Venice of the Orient.

They had booked into a hotel. And they had celebrated their escape with a champagne dinner sent up to them. Despite his heavy loneliness, despite the anguish he felt at April Rose's death, which he knew would stay with him forever, Bolan felt good to be warring against a part of that vast enemy he had fingered as the perpetrator of the crime. Evil threatened to devour every last spark of goodness in his world, but Bolan would never be extinguished. He shone all the brighter as he set life and limb against the stinking morass of his global enemy. Each mission would chop into the foulness of the world's cancer, reclaim a path for civilization and carve a route toward the righteous avenging of his beloved April.

Each mission was like fresh oxygen to a man dedicated to taking out every single one of the traitors, assassins, commandos, psychos and punks behind the murder of his true love.

Now Bolan stood by an open window, waiting for Olga Wilson, the League president in Washington, to return his call.

They had arrived in the city hours earlier, getting out of the Buick on the outskirts to make their entry by water. It was much more discreet than getting out of a car in brightly lit downtown. In their outfits they would have caused suspicion.

They had gone first to the Khmer Rouge legation, where a doctor treated Eng's wound while Bolan developed the photos and dubbed the cassettes. They also changed into fresh clothes from their suitcases, which they had left in the legation when they sailed for Cambodia.

Now Bolan was wearing a suit. He wriggled his toes in his black shoes. He was still enjoying the feel of shoes that fitted. Major Karkor's pair had been murder to wear.

The telephone rang.

"Hello, Mr. Bolan," said a distant voice. "Olga Wilson. I just received your message. When did you return?"

"A few hours ago."

"Any luck?"

"There is a resort and there are American tourists in it," Bolan replied, using prearranged code words. "I have thirty-five names."

"Is, I mean, among the names is ...." The sentence trailed off expectantly.

"I'm sorry, no. But there is another resort. It's to the north in a next-door country. Your husband might be there."

"You mean there are actually two?"

"So it appears. The information is from a reliable source. I also learned something else—our management has been telling us stories. They know of the resorts. They even know who the tourists are."

"Say that again," Wilson said.

Bolan repeated and went on. "The reason they are pretending they don't know is that they don't want to pay a bonus, which the travel office is requesting. It's quite a large bonus.''

"That's very interesting, Mr. Bolan. But were you able to bring back any documentation?''

"I have pictures of the resort and some of the tourists,'' Bolan said. "Also, their voices.''

"You were able to speak to them?''

"Yeah.''

"Did anybody mention or know of ....'' Once again the words trailed off expectantly.

"It wasn't that kind of a conversation,'' Bolan said. "There was no privacy, and they didn't know who I was.''

"Mr. Bolan, this is wonderful,'' she said, personal disappointment giving way to official enthusiasm. "When can we expect your arrival?''

"I'm sending the material by air express tonight. There's a plane leaving in two hours. I'll call you later with the waybill number.''

"And yourself? When can we expect you to arrive?''

"I cannot tell you that.''

"Mr. Bolan, the feeling at the League is that we should let our management handle this. Now that we have documentation, we have an excellent case. But we'd have to publicize it, and what better publicity than yourself. We need you in Washington.''

"I can't publicize, you know that. It's out of the question.''

"I don't mean publicly. I plan to hold a dinner for a few senators and a few newspapermen. It will be strictly off the record.''

"No. I should concentrate on putting together the next expedition,'' Bolan growled. "We don't have much time. The other side knows I visited them and will in all probability take steps to organize a welcome. We have to beat them to it. We have to move fast.''

"We will explain that to the management.''

"The management doesn't have people, Mrs. Wilson. We have.''

"Of course they have people, Mr. Bolan. You know, the ones from the Halls of Montezuma.'' She meant the U.S. Marines.

"They will never agree to use them.''

"Mr. Bolan, much as I appreciate your opinion, it *is* the League that is paying for you. And it is the feeling of the committee that you will be more useful to us in Washington than in Bangkok. I therefore suggest that we terminate this argument and that you get on the next plane. Are you all right for money?''

"Yes.''

"Then please be on that plane. And please call us when you get to San Francisco or Los Angeles, whichever, so we can arrange to have someone meet you at the airport in Washington.''

"You realize, Mrs. Wilson,'' Bolan said, trying one last time, "that if we. . . .''

"Mr. Bolan, please.''

"Goodbye,'' he spat, hanging up.

He went back to the window. Management! Who needed Washington? This was going to be a fiasco, he was sure of it. It was going to be another raid like that one on Hanoi Hilton. By the time the expedition finally got off, the POW camp was empty. That's what happened when people fought wars by committee.

Bolan gazed at the pulsing city, then went to the phone and called the airport. Next he walked to his bedroom to pack a bag. When he was through, he went to Eng's bedroom. The side lamp was on, but she was sleeping. For a while he stood by the bedside watching her. She slept with her eyelids half closed as did a lot of Asiatics, and it gave her a mysterious, evil air.

A she-devil, Bolan remembered Parong had called her, and there was quite a bit of that in her, he had to admit. The face was devilish and the woman was ruthless. On the other hand she was not devious, at least not with him.

Suddenly her eyes fluttered open, surveying him. "What's wrong?"

"I have to go away," he said.

"Did you write the report?"

He nodded. "Your copy is on the dining table with the other things."

He headed for the door. Before he reached it the light went off and he heard her turn on her side. It was as if he had already ceased to exist in her life.

It took him forty minutes to get to the airport. At the airline counter a crowd of elderly people was lining up to check in. He joined the line.

Finally he got to the counter. "My name is Bolan," he said. "I have a reservation." It was a pleasure to use his real name, it was a symbol of his freedom, and he would use it defiantly, at every opportunity. At worst it meant nothing, at best it was a calling card for his enemies.

"Bolan...Bolan," the clerk said, checking a list. "When did you make it, sir?"

"An hour or so ago."

The clerk picked up the telephone and made a call. After a brief conversation he cupped the receiver. "They're checking."

The wait seemed interminable. The travelers around him began to mutter.

"Mr. Bolan?" said a Thai voice. "These gentlemen are from the American embassy and they would like to speak to you."

Bolan turned to see the speaker indicating three men. They were embassy all right, he could tell by their clothes—the political office of the embassy to be exact. Every profession has its own style and the coolly sophisticated clothes of this pair spelled CIA. Both had a hand in their raincoat pockets. They were young, clean cut and polite.

"After you, Mr. Bolan, please," one of them said.

At sea it had been easy to choose whether to fight or surrender, but here he was hemmed in by a crowd of senior citizens. He could see Thai plainclothesmen by the door, and saw one move next to the clerk behind the counter.

Bolan picked up his flight bag and headed for the door, followed by the agents.

"Where are we going?" he asked as they entered a limousine.

"The embassy," replied one of them.

"Any particular reason?"

"The official one is murder."

THE MAN STANDING BEHIND THE DESK nodded a greeting. He was tall, blond and wore a black dinner jacket with a red carnation in the lapel.

"Jeff Svenson," he said, introducing himself. He motioned Bolan to a chair and sat down in turn. "I was at a party," he said, gesturing at his evening clothes. He reached for the phone. "Would you like some coffee?"

"Sure," Bolan said, eyes sweeping the office. It was a plush bunker, windowless, with a low ceiling. The walls were covered in soundproofing material, the leather of the soundproofing matching the leather of the furniture.

Svenson ordered the coffee and replaced the phone. He pushed his chair back and crossed his legs.

"How was Cambodia?" he asked.

"First things first," Bolan said. "Why am I here? Your man said the charge was murder."

Svenson dismissed the subject with a wave of the hand. He had the ease of manner of a career diplomat. "That was merely a pretext. Your killing the mole in Washington is of no interest to this station. Our real interest is your Cambodian trip."

"You still haven't answered my question," Bolan said. "I want to know why I was abducted."

"We'll get around to that over coffee." Svenson's voice was hardening.

Bolan gave a resigned shrug. He had been up for two nights and did not need to argue. "What do you want to know?" he asked.

"From the beginning. Say we start with how you crossed into Cambodia."

Bolan recounted the mission the way it had happened.

"How did you find out I was in Bangkok?" he asked in conclusion.

"Langley called us. They monitored Olga Wilson's conversation with you."

"You spy in the States now?" Bolan said.

The man ignored the remark. "Your POW evidence is political dynamite," he said. "There's no way Washington can meet Hanoi's ransom demands. A precedent would be set for every gook from Arafat to the Sandinistas. Next thing you know the Libyans will be asking for a billion in return for the spy ship."

"Spy ship?"

"Happened last week," Svenson said. "One of our

ships got caught in Libyan waters. We're trying for an exchange—the ship in return for a Libyan hit crew we're holding.''

There was a knock on the door and a liveried Thai butler wheeled in the coffee trolley. Svenson dismissed him and poured the coffee himself.

"Not only is your POW evidence dynamite internationally, it's even bigger dynamite domestically. Blowing the lid on the ransom demands will seriously embarrass the administration. Can you imagine the howl that will go up? The government lying to the country, saying it knows of no POWs, when all the time it had a list of them from the Vietnamese themselves? It'll be another Watergate.''

"So that's why you picked me up?"

"I'm afraid you're in for a period of prolonged seclusion,'' Svenson said gravely.

"The League is expecting me in Washington,'' Bolan said.

"You won't be the first crook who took their money and disappeared. Look,'' said Svenson heatedly. "I also fought in Vietnam. You think I enjoy having to put you away? I would like to see those men freed just as much as you, but one has to be a realist. Sometimes a few have to be sacrificed for the good of the majority.''

"I understand,'' Bolan said, putting his cup down. He wanted to terminate the conversation. It depressed him intensely.

Svenson sensed the down mood and he picked up the telephone to call in the escorts.

"Take Mr. Bolan back to his quarters,'' he told them. To Bolan he said. "I'll send you up some books. Anything special you might like?''

"Yeah,'' Bolan said. *"The Ugly American.''*

THEY TOOK HIM UPSTAIRS and locked him in a small apartment. The window looked out onto a park. He was in a villa in the eastern part of town, a U.S. embassy annex.

He went to the window and opened it. It was dawn, the air fresh, the sky streaked violet. He heard the purr of scooters as early risers headed for work.

The sky, the fresh air, the scooters—they all spelled freedom.

He was a prisoner.

He began pacing the room like an angry trapped tiger.

After an hour of pacing, he stood still. Then calmly he went to the telephone on a table in a corner of the apartment and called the clean-cut young man downstairs.

"This is Bolan. Who's the chief of station here?"

"Mr. Balzani," the guard replied.

"What time does he get in?"

"Normally about ten o'clock."

"Give him a message from me. Tell him I request an appointment with him any time after twelve noon. Specify that it must be after twelve, not before."

"I will pass on the message, sir."

Bolan replaced the receiver and went to bed.

THE CHIEF OF STATION, a small man with a handlebar mustache, observed Bolan with a guarded air. Instinct—or was it Bolan's confidence?—told him to expect trouble.

"You wished to see me?" he asked.

"I have some news for you," Bolan replied. "If by six o'clock tonight a certain party does not hear from me, a copy of the POW material will be sent to the League of Families."

"You made copies?"

"Yes."

"I see."

"I should tell you that the material will be routed in such a way that no one can intercept it."

"I see," Balzani repeated, twirling his mustache pensively. "Why are you telling us this now? Why did you not tell Svenson?"

"The party in question was staying the night in my hotel suite. Svenson would have raided the suite and confiscated the material. Now it is too late. The party has gone. Noon was checkout time."

Balzani picked up the telephone. "Find out how many occupants were in Mr. Bolan's suite." He replaced the receiver.

They waited in silence, Bolan's eyes burning into the chief of station across from him, who gazed out at the branches beyond the window. Neither made any attempt at conversation.

The telephone rang. "Yes? Thanks." Balzani turned to Bolan. "What do you propose?"

"In return for the second POW package, the CIA agrees to undertake a rescue operation to free the POWs," Bolan said.

The twirling stopped abruptly. Balzani brought out a pipe and stuffed it with tobacco.

"The actual fighting will be carried out by the Khmer Rouge," Bolan continued. "The CIA will provide logistic support."

"And who will command this rescue?"

"I will. The plan will be basically the same as the one I proposed to the League. The cost will be a million dollars."

Balzani lit his pipe. "A million dollars is a lot of money," he said. "Nice bit of blackmail."

"Yeah," Bolan agreed.

"Of course I will have to discuss all this with Langley."

"Of course. The deadline is six." Bolan rose. "I'll be upstairs if you want me."

SOME TIME LATER Bolan was awakened by knocking on the door. It was Balzani, come to inform him that he was no longer a prisoner.

Langley had accepted his proposal.

The mission was back on the rails.

9

The Huey gunship skimmed the treetops, flying low to avoid Vietnamese radar. On board, Bolan and Eng pored over a 1:50,000-scale map spread on their knees. They were returning to Cambodia. Once again they were dressed in black fighting suits, but now they wore red scarves. On the floor lay their weapons, Morse radio pack and a haversack full of money.

"Why don't you want to land in the village?" Eng shouted over the din of the rotor blades.

"Too dangerous," Bolan shouted back. "They might take us for Vietnamese."

"We can drop a message first."

Bolan shook his head. "We could still be hit while flying over. All it takes is one bullet."

The gunner on their right shouted. "Village coming up at two o'clock."

"That must be Tram Yo," Eng said.

A Montagnard hamlet went by, barracklike huts hugging the side of a hill. People waved to them. Thirty years of war had taught them that it always paid to be friendly to helicopters, regardless who was flying them.

"Yes, it's Tram Yo," Eng said. She pointed it out to Bolan on the map.

Bolan lifted the receiver off the hook at his back. "We're dead on course," he told the pilot.

"Thanks," came the reply. Flying so low, the pilot could not see many landmarks and had to rely on Bolan and Eng to guide him.

Bolan returned to the map.

"Or we could land here," Eng said. "There is a clearing. Only an hour's march from the village."

Bolan picked up the telephone again. "Got an LZ for you." He gave the pilot the coordinates and hung up.

Eng put the map away and shivered. "It's cold," she said.

Bolan put an arm around her. It was not the arm of a lover; it was the warm arm of friendship. They had become friends. Good friends.

The process had begun the previous day at his hotel suite when Eng turned up asking if she could spend the evening with him. The legation was giving a party, and she did not want to be present. A widow was always thought of as easy prey.

Which is how Bolan found out that Eng had been married. Her husband was the man who originally commanded her maquis. She took over after his death. He had been betrayed to the Vietnamese by the brothel keeper, which was why Eng killed the brothel keeper's husband.

Bolan took her out to dinner, then he took her back to the legation, only to find out that the party was still in progress. Eng did not want to go into the house, so Bolan suggested she sleep in her old bedroom at the hotel. He had the same suite.

They talked and talked. At one point, Eng began to cry. Later, he would find out this had been her first wedding anniversary. He comforted her with words, and their bond of friendship became real.

"Landing zone," the gunner called out. A moment later they flew over a clearing.

The helicopter banked and the pilot began circling, the gunners on the sides leaning out, inspecting the ground. Bolan and Eng put on their gear and took hold of their weapons. The helicopter passed then returned, coming to hover above the clearing. Slowly it came down and touched ground.

"Thanks for the ride," Bolan said into the telephone. He gave the nearest gunner a thumbs-up sign and led Eng out of the helicopter.

Crouched over, hands holding their bush hats in the blast of air, they ran through swirling dust and flying leaves. When they reached the trees, the helicopter was rising, turning at the same time. The gunner waved to them and the gunship flew off. The clearing was plunged into silence.

"Home sweet home," Bolan muttered, looking around.

They set out for the village, first going cross-country, then taking a trail.

They came to a ravine with a suspension bridge hung across. As they approached the bridge, men appeared from the tree line on the other side. Bolan dropped to a knee and brought up his weapon.

But it was P'um, leading a patrol to find out why the helicopter had come. Seeing it return so quickly, they assumed it had dropped off a Vietnamese reconnaissance team.

The warriors took a break to catch up on each others' news.

P'um told them that soon after Bolan and Eng had left the hotel to go to the POW camp, the Vietnamese police arrived and began searching the hotel for the missing Tartar and his wife. Tipped off by a domestic, P'um stole a jeep and fled.

"There's a reward out for us," P'um said.

"Yes, we heard," Eng said. "Twenty thousand riels."

"They've doubled it. It's forty thousand now. And there is a rumor that reinforcements are on the way. I think a search-and-destroy mission is being planned to please the Russians. They are very upset that the colonel and the major were killed."

"Any idea of what they think the false Major Karkor was up to?" Bolan asked.

"They seem uncertain. There are two theories. One is that it was an attempt to free the prisoners and that for some inexplicable reason the attempt failed. Another is that you were reconnoitering the camp in preparation for a rescue attempt. Either way, they are not taking chances. In Yen Sai the curfew has been extended by four hours and there are more patrols. In the fort, guards have been strengthened and all Cambodian personnel have been removed. They don't trust the Cambodians. The cooks, cleaners and maintenance personnel are all Vietnamese now."

In the sky, a Russian-made Vietnamese transport plane droned toward Phnom Penh. For all Bolan knew, it could be bringing reinforcements from Hanoi.

"We can't attack the fort head-on," Eng said. "The Vietnamese would massacre us."

"I need to get a message through to the prisoners," Bolan said slowly, looking into the distance.

P'um turned to Bolan. "I have a contact who accepts bribes, a Veitnamese officer who can do that for you. His name is Lok. He had an affair with the military governor's wife, and a fellow officer is blackmailing him. He always needs money."

"Contact the guy," Bolan said. "We'll pay any amount he wants."

"Any amount?" P'um asked.

"Damn near any amount," Bolan said. "This is our last chance."

UNDER THE MOONLIGHT, they awaited the arrival of the lieutenant. The forest was hushed, the road deserted. Bolan and P'um stood on the edge of a clearing in the shadow of some trees. Their horses were tied nearby. In the middle of the clearing stood a pyramid of skulls; the rendezvous was a former Khmer Rouge killground. A plaque on the enclosure stated that two thousand people had been clubbed to death there. The kill teams had been saving on ammunition.

"You've dealt with him often?" Bolan whispered.

"A few times."

From afar droned the sound of an engine. It grew louder and a pair of headlights pierced the night. As it neared, Bolan saw that it was an amphibious jeep. The vehicle turned off the road into the clearing. The driver switched off the engine but left the lights on.

"Why are so many skulls cracked?" a voice called out. It was the password.

"That's not Lok," P'um whispered urgently. "I know Lok's voice."

"Answer anyway," Bolan said.

"The people were clubbed," P'um called out.

"Come out where I can see you," the driver ordered.

"Who are you?" P'um asked. They remained in the shadows. "You're not the lieutenant."

"I'm the lieutenant's driver," came the reply. "The meeting has been moved. I will drive you."

"Where?"

"Near the coast. Only a five-minute drive."

"Why the change?"

"The lieutenant doesn't trust long noses. You might have men hidden. You coming?"

P'um looked questioningly at Bolan.

"We risk it," Bolan said. "We don't have much choice."

They came up to the jeep and climbed into the back. The driver turned the vehicle around, and they went bumping along the potholed road toward the coast. A mile down they turned onto a paved stretch of the coastal highway, driving away from Yen Sai.

Two miles farther they turned onto a side road that ran parallel to a canal. They came to a compound that was evidently a brick factory. They drove past mounds of bricks and pulled up outside a house on stilts.

They got out and the driver led them up the steps and knocked on the door. It was opened by a handsome, slightly effeminate man in civilian clothes who had the unmistakable bearing of an officer.

"Good evening, gentlemen," he said. "Come in." He added with a smile. "I see you are armed."

They entered a cluttered office lit by lanterns. The driver remained outside. The officer motioned them to chairs facing a desk. He sat behind it. As he retrieved a cigarette smoldering at the end of a holder in an ashtray, his eyes swept Bolan appraisingly.

"Did you bring the money?" Lok asked.

Bolan tapped the haversack by his feet.

"I would like to count it," Lok said.

Bolan opened the bag and placed five bundles of notes on the desk. Each contained a hundred twenty-dollar bills. "Ten thousand," Bolan said.

Lok counted each packet. "Ten thousand," he agreed.

He put the money in a drawer. "What exactly do you want me to do?"

Bolan brought out a letter from inside his shirt.

"I want you to deliver this to an American prisoner at the fort," he said. "His name is Major Cosgrove. The letter must be delivered tomorrow. Inside is a receipt that Major Cosgrove must sign and return to you. When you give me the receipt I will pay you the remaining ten thousand dollars."

Lok raised the cigarette holder to his mouth. He held it from underneath, a style affected by Vietnamese intellectuals. Eyes on Bolan, he took a long, slow drag. "What is in that letter?"

"A personal message," Bolan said.

"How personal?"

"Very personal," Bolan replied. He held up the reverse side and pointed to a seal. "If this seal is broken, the major will not sign the receipt."

Lok tapped the cigarette in the ashtray. Next to the ashtray stood a small skull, a baby's.

"I think I should read the letter before I deliver it," Lok announced.

"Out of the question," Bolan said. "The message is personal."

A playful smile crossed Lok's lips. "A secret?"

"A secret," Bolan repeated.

Lok considered this. "Frankly, I don't think I can deliver a message the contents of which I don't know."

Bolan glanced at P'um.

"He's reneging," P'um said. "I told him the message was personal, and he agreed to deliver without reading it."

"I agreed to deliver a personal message," Lok said. "I did not agree to deliver a secret message." He gave Bolan another appraising look.

"You're playing with words," P'um said angrily. "What does it matter, secret or personal? You agreed to deliver it unread."

"I agreed because you made me understand it was a family matter," Lok retorted.

"He's lying," P'um said to Bolan. "I never said anything about a family matter."

"The seal would suggest it is a military matter," Lok said. He looked at Bolan. "Is it a military matter?"

"Yes," Bolan replied.

Lok stubbed out the cigarette and put the holder aside. "To deliver a message on a military matter is a risky business," he said, looking steadily at Bolan.

Bolan preferred to negotiate with a gun, especially when the numbers were falling. In two hours' time he had to be at a drop zone to pick up supplies for the assault on the fort. They were running out of time.

"Listen, Lok," he said. "You either play the game by the rules, or you never play again."

"For the risk involved," Lok said. "I think delivery of such a message will cost a minimum of forty thousand dollars."

Lok lit another cigarette, inserted it into the holder and took a long drag. He leaned back in his chair and glanced at his watch.

Realization exploded in Bolan's head. The glance at the watch confirmed it. It was the glance of a man who was waiting for something. The whole meeting was phony. Bribery deals did not go on like this, they were quick and to the point.

"The deal is off," Bolan said, rising. "Give me the money."

"Sit down," Lok said.

"I said the deal is off," Bolan repeated. He turned to P'um. "Get the driver."

Out of the corner of his eye Bolan saw Lok reaching into the drawer that contained the money. Bolan's hand swept the desk top, sending the lamp flying. It crashed to the floor, spilling kerosene. There was a loud whoosh as the kerosene ignited. A moment later the desk was engulfed by flames.

Through the flames Bolan saw Lok pointing a gun at him. He threw himself sideways as Lok fired, then rolled as Lok fired again. P'um's AK-47 filled the office with its roar. Lok spun and crashed to the ground in a bloody heap.

From outside came the sound of boots on steps. The door flew open and the driver appeared, an assault rifle tracking, his eyes darting nervously. The AK-47 roared again and blew him back.

"Start the jeep," Bolan shouted over the crackle of flames.

P'um ran out while Bolan went to the drawer and loaded the haversack with bills. Flames rose all around him. As he was stuffing the last wad into the satchel, a searing pain made him look down. His trouser leg was on fire. He beat it out with the haversack.

Bolan ran out of the house. P'um was behind the wheel, the jeep's engine idling. Bolan threw his gun and haversack into the back seat and jumped in. "Go. Go!" he shouted.

The amphibious vehicle shot forward, past the mounds of bricks, past the gate, onto the road. They saw headlights approaching on the coastal road from Yen Sai. One pair, two pairs, three. Armored cars.

Now Bolan knew he was right. The meeting had been a trap to collect $20,000 dollars in bribe money and

$3,000 in reward money. Without having to betray his own kind, Lok would be a rich man.

The armored cars were approaching the junction to the brick factory road.

P'um eased his foot off the accelerator. The jeep slowed down.

"Use the canal," Bolan shouted.

"I don't know how to drive in water."

"Lever to the right," Bolan instructed. "When we enter water, pull it."

The headlights of the armored cars drew nearer, speeding toward them. With fifty meters to go before collision, P'um drove the jeep off the road. They bumped down the steep embankment of the canal and splashed into the water. P'um pulled the lever, transferring the power from the wheels to the rear propeller, and the jeep purred upstream.

The armored cars screeched to a halt. A powerful searchlight came on, sweeping the canal. Bolan ducked, but too late. His face was illuminated and gunfire filled the air. Soldiers sat on all three cars.

Bolan raised his AKM and aimed for the light. A line of red tracers hit the searchlight. Glass tinkled, smoke puffed, and darkness returned amidst shouts.

The first armored car took off toward the factory; the third one began the difficult process of turning, while the middle one swung its gun turret.

The cannon on the turret roared, and a fountain of water geysered from the canal. The jeep swayed, buffeted by waves.

"Get back on the road," Bolan shouted.

P'um jerked the wheel and they headed for shore, Bolan firing at soldiers running on the road after them. The front wheels hit the incline at the side of the canal. P'um pushed the lever and the wheels bit the surface. They bumped up the embankment out of the cannon's range of fire—the third car had blocked its path.

The amphibious jeep bounced onto the road and sped off. The third armored car followed in hot pursuit.

Tires screaming, the jeep turned onto the coastal road. The armored car followed.

A pair of headlights appeared ahead. As they came closer, Bolan could see it was a truck filled with troops. He fired a burst as the vehicle passed. There was the sound of exploding tires and the truck swerved wildly.

The armored car drove off the road to avoid the truck. It must have stalled, because the light from the headlights remained stationary. But not for long. As the jeep turned onto the forest road, Bolan saw the armored car following them again.

The jeep sped on the forest road, bouncing high in the air each time it hit a pothole. The holes slowed them down. The armored car turned in after them. Now that they were off the highway the armored car opened fire.

A shell from the cannon hit the road ahead of them, a second exploded against a tree on the right, a third fell short. The potholes made aiming difficult. In the back of the jeep, Bolan returned fire, aiming for the headlights and the tires, but mesh grilles covered the lights and armor-plating protected the tires.

The distance between the two vehicles narrowed. The machine gun on the armored car opened up, and bullets thudded into the jeep. A bullet pierced the windshield from behind, crystallizing it. P'um punched a hole so he could see. The smell of gasoline filled the air. The tank had been hit.

"We're better off on foot," Bolan shouted.

"We're nearly there," P'um yelled back.

The clearing came into view and he swung the wheel. The jeep screeched to a halt and they jumped out, leaving the engine running and sprinting for the tree line.

The armored car roared into the clearing just as they were leaving it.

The cannon fired. A shell exploded over their heads. The blast smashed them to the ground. But within seconds they had themselves up and, ignoring the tracer bullets that churned the foliage, were running for the horses.

They were free men, galloping through the forest, the gunfire receding behind them.

But they had lost their only chance to contact the prisoners. And contacting the prisoners was the only way to arrange for the gates of the fort to be opened for them.

Now Bolan and his fighters would have to smash their way in on their own.

10

The DC-3 roared over the valley, the winking light on its belly glowing red. Bolan watched as the dark shapes of falling crates were followed by blossoming parachutes.

Having disgorged its load of supplies the aircraft circled above the field that was strewn with crates and containers, waiting for confirmation.

"Tell them a whole crate is defective," Bolan said. "Almost cost us."

"I'll pass it on. Anything else?"

"Yeah, where's Hippocrates?" The dispatch of a doctor was one of the conditions set by the Khmer Rouge for the assault on the fort.

"Stand by," the pilot replied. There was a moment of silence and he said, "Nighthawk? Alpha says Piper had a breakdown. Trouble's been fixed and they're on the way. Should be here in twenty minutes or so. Alpha asks for confirmation that you'll be on hand to receive him."

"Confirmed," Bolan said.

The plane flew off and Bolan moved to where the crates were being unpacked. A carnival atmosphere prevailed as the supplies were inspected.

In addition to weapons and food, the CIA had sent such luxuries as coffee, chocolate, aspirins, laundry detergent and American cigarettes. Many of the items were unobtainable in war-torn Cambodia, others hard to get. Morale boosters, the CIA called them.

Bolan told Eng about the doctor. "I'll catch up with you later."

"Shall I leave some men?" she asked.

"No, but I'll need two extra horses. One for the doctor and one pack pony in case he's got gear."

"You'd better have some men," she said. "There may be Moulaka soldiers in the area."

A few minutes later a team of Montagnard riders appeared with a couple of extra horses. He led them back to his slope, and they sat down to wait. The villagers continued loading. When everything was done they formed a column and moved on into the night.

"Excuse me, chief," said one of the guerrillas. "Is it true that someone will open the gates of the fort for us?"

"Where did you hear this?" Bolan asked.

"People are talking."

"That's the general idea, yes."

A moment of silence followed. "Is it a secret how this will be done?"

"Yes, it's a secret," Bolan said, still pondering the problem of how he was going to get those gates open.

One of the guerrillas called out. A flashing light was moving in the western sky.

The men threw more branches on the fires, illuminating the valley. The radio came to life. It was the Piper with the doctor. The plane was flying low and Bolan caught sight of a figure standing on a jump stand next to the wing. The Piper flew out and circled, gaining height. On the third circle the figure detached itself and a parachute opened.

Bolan watched the doctor descend. He was harnessed to a para-commando type parachute that could be steered. At the back of the canopy was a slit through which air could escape and which acted as a jet, propelling the parachute down at a speed of fifteen kilometers an hour. By pulling toggles attached to the risers, the parachutist could close part of the jet, maneuvering himself in the direction he wanted.

The doctor turned from side to side, one moment riding with the wind, the next against it, constantly adjusting his position for a pinpoint landing.

As he watched, a tingling sensation started at the back of Bolan's neck. He had it. The answer to the problem of how to open the gate.

11

In the shade of a flame tree, Bolan tapped feverishly on the Morse key of his radio transmitter. It was morning, the sun was shining, the sky blue. He sat at a table, earphones on. Over his shoulder stood a group of guerrillas, all eager to know what would be the CIA's reaction to Bolan's battle plan.

Originally Bolan had intended to make a solo parachute jump into the fort, but since then, new information had come his way, making it possible to plan a much more ambitious operation. He learned from the doctor that the CIA had a large quantity of para-commando chutes, along with a roomful of skydiving equipment. And from Eng he found out there were many ex-parachutists in the proletarian brigade.

That meant there were equipment and manpower for an airborne insert in force. Instead of one, several gates could be opened, speeding the entry of the assault force into the fort. Second, a strike could be mounted simultaneously against the four corner towers, neutralizing their machine guns, thus limiting casualties.

In his message to the CIA, Bolan was proposing a clandestine drop, one from very high up, so the guards at the fort would not be tipped off by the sound of the plane. To reduce the risk of discovery, he planned to free-fall most of the way and open the parachutes at the last moment.

The group around Bolan were the men who would make the jump. There were eighteen of them: Cambodian mercenaries who had deserted a Vietnamese parachute regiment. The group included many experienced men. Some had served in the Cambodian royal army and had jumped with Americans. Two were real veterans, ex-members of a French foreign legion parachutist regiment.

They watched Bolan in silence, the atmosphere heavy with expectation. Even if the CIA approved, the operation might not be feasible if the weather was poor. Visibility had to be good, and the winds could not be too strong.

A final staccato burst through the transmitter resounded as Bolan signed off. He switched the set to receive and heard Bangkok acknowledge receipt of the message. He slid off one earphone, leaving the other on, pushed his chair away from the table and leaned back.

"Now we wait," he announced to the group.

"How soon before they answer?" someone asked.

"Twenty minutes, half an hour."

Someone passed a pack of Salem cigarettes, which had arrived with the night drop, and they lit up. Then began the sort of banter common to men eager for action.

"How high will we go to jump, chief?"

"Depends on the plane. They'll probably send us a C-47," Bolan said. "That has a ceiling of twenty-four thousand feet or about seven thousand meters. I guess we'll go out at between six and seven thousand meters."

"Will we be jumping directly over the fort?"

"No, they'd hear us. We'll be jumping out at sea."

"Over the sea?" said a young man, eyes widening. He had never seen the sea.

"The prevailing winds come from the sea this time of the

year," Bolan said. "We have to jump with the wind. But that could change. The day I arrived in this country I ran into a storm with offshore winds. We won't know for certain until the last moment."

"How far out at sea?" the young man continued.

"Depends on the wind," an older man in the group answered for Bolan. "What do you figure, chief, one kilometer horizontally for every two down?"

"Uh-huh."

"That's without wind," another observed.

Bolan nodded.

"Where will we board the plane?"

"In a valley two ranges from here," Bolan said. "The ground is hard enough to take a C-47."

"We'll dress on the airstrip, won't we, chief?" said the older man.

"If the CIA agrees to the operation, they'll put the gear on the plane for us."

"Have you done much parachuting, chief?" asked a new voice.

Bolan nodded.

On the parade ground nearby, units were forming and being given their machine orders. The assault force was leaving in small groups to avoid being spotted from the air by the Vietnamese. The ones going overland were the first to leave. The bulk of the force would go later by river, using bamboo rafts.

This was one hell of an army for a commander whose status was fugitive. Bolan listened to the orders being given in the distance and brooded on his fate.

He knew he would get the go-ahead for this ambitious attack. His instinct had already told him that the weather and the availability of transport and equipment would all be favorable.

The war was on again.

He looked hard at the Oriental fighting men who surrounded him.

Just like old times....

12

The C-47's engine revved, the aircraft trembling from the strain. It would have to be a quick takeoff—the strip was short and at the far end was a forest. In the cabin, Bolan and his men shook from the vibrations as they braced themselves with the aid of overhead straps. They sat facing one another on canvas benches, nineteen men dressed in black, faces camouflaged with paint, weapons equipped with silencers.

It was 2205 hours. Winds were easterly at five to eight kilometers per hour. The airborne assault was under way.

The engines reached a crescendo, the plane lumbered forward. The flaming torches, held by women to mark the runway, flashed by the portholes with increasing speed. The torches blurred and the aircraft rose. It banked, then straightened out. Moonlight streamed into the cabin as they headed for the sea.

Bolan hooked his strap and went into the pilot's cabin.

"The radio?" the pilot asked.

"Yeah," Bolan said. He gave the frequency and the pilot adjusted the selector.

"Use the wall set," the pilot said.

Bolan unhooked it. "Nighthawk to White Lotus."

The earpiece was full of static. "White Lotus speaking," a woman's voice said.

"We're en route," Bolan said. "Are you in position?"

"Yes, we are," Eng replied.

Bolan asked the pilot to put him on another frequency and unhooked again. "Nighthawk to Speedbird."

"Speedbird."

"Are you in position?"

"Affirmative." It was the CIA hovercraft that would evacuate the prisoners. It was waiting a hundred kilometers up the coast in Thai waters.

"We're airborne and on our way. Over and out."

Bolan returned to his seat. Bolan took out a drawing of the fort and studied it for the last time, with the aid of a penlight. The sketch had been sent to Eng by her agent in town—a drawing based on details given in an interview with some Cambodian domestics who had been employed there. It showed the side gates, the entrance to the mine tunnel, the garrison's quarters and the communications room.

The aircraft climbed the sky over the sea. Bolan listened to the drone of the engines, head tilted back, eyes closed.

The dispatcher went by, hand raised showing three fingers, and the cabin stirred to life. They unplugged the oxygen leads from the plane's supply and plugged them into their own individual oxygen bottles, which they carried at the waist. The jumpers strapped on their leather helmets and put on their goggles. Some men tightened the laces on their jump boots.

They rose, forming one line, and Bolan inspected them. He checked their parachutes and made sure their equipment was secure. In addition to their Sterling submachine guns, they carried ammunition, grenades of all kinds and demolition satchels.

When he was through, he took his place at the head of the line.

The dispatcher spoke to the pilot via the speaker in the side of his mask. He trailed wire to the intercom. Off a hook he took a small blackboard with a reading lamp. He wrote on it in chalk and turned on the light. He walked past the masked faces, holding up the board so everyone could see it.

The board gave the latest weather information: visibility was still one hundred percent, but the wind had increased and changed direction slightly. It was now southeasterly, ten to fifteen kilometers per hour.

The men exchanged glances. The new figures meant they could not overshoot their target. Before, they could have backtracked using the propulsion of their parachutes. Not anymore. The wind was now strong enough to neutralize that.

The dispatcher opened the door, and cold air flooded into the cabin. He motioned to Bolan to take position: Bolan stepped into the doorway, his gloved hands gripping the sides, wind tearing at his clothes. Outside, the night stretched into infinity.

Bolan looked at the altimeter on his right wrist. They were flying at just over 6,000 meters, 900 below the plane's ceiling. He looked at the compass on his left wrist. They were flying south, parallel to the coast.

A buzzer went off, a hand slapped his back and he dived into the void. The slipstream swept him. The next thing he knew he was spread-eagled on his stomach, floating. The only sound was the flapping of his clothes and the whistling of the wind in the earholes of his helmet. He tilted his head and looked over his shoulder. A stack of fluttering shapes followed him.

A cloud rushed up and they were enveloped in a cold, damp fog. Bolan's goggles misted over. Then they were out of it, back in the warm, bright night, but his goggles were still clouded. He brought his hands up, but made sure he did not lose his balance and go into a spin. He pulled the goggles briefly away from his face. The maneuver cleared them.

He spread his arms again and turned his attention to the target. He could see it quite clearly now, the lit-up mine and darker fort. He decided the fort was a little too far to their right. He dipped his arm and shoulder to the right to move himself in that direction. Again he looked over his shoulder. The others followed as if on command.

Wind whistling in their ears, clothes flapping, the vanguard of the night's assault hurtled through the air around one hundred seventy kilometers an hour.

Bolan glanced at his altimeter again. They were at 3,000 meters. The fort was still a little too far to the right, but he decided not to dip anymore. They would correct their path when they used their parachutes. With the wind the way it was, better to be a little short than to overshoot.

At 2100 meters Bolan went off oxygen. Again, using both hands to maintain balance, he lowered the mask over his neck and cut off the oxygen supply. He could have left it on—it had a seven-minute supply—but he did not want to waste it. He could use oxygen in lieu of a gas mask on the ground.

Fifteen hundred meters.

He glanced over his shoulder and saw silk streaming and canopies blooming. Now only four of them were free-falling: himself, the two former legionnaires and one of the royalists. It was part of the plan. Team number one—Bolan and the other free-fallers—would land on the ramparts and knock out the towers. Teams number two and three would land a few seconds later on the parade ground.

At 900 meters, Bolan reached for the rip cord and opened the chute. For a moment the world blurred. Deceleration at that instant is so great—from one hundred seventy kilometers an hour to twenty-five—that rookies often passed out for a second or two. Bolan stayed conscious, feeling every bit of the neck-twisting, back-wrenching tug.

He pushed the goggles over his forehead and reached for the toggles on the risers. He steered for the northeastern tower. A former legionnaire stuck close behind him, going for the northwestern tower. The two towers were the most important of the four because they controlled access to the two side gates in the northern wall through which the main assault force would enter.

Not many lights were on in the buildings, indicating most people were asleep. The parade ground was in total darkness and so were the ramparts. The arc lights in the towers were trained on the ground outside the fort.

The northern rampart drew nearer. Bolan constantly pulled on the toggles. To the right, to the left, going backward, going forward, sideways. He could feel sweat building up on his forehead from the strain of concentration. The rampart was no more than eight feet wide—not much room. He had to make a standup landing. If he rolled, he would go over the side and meet certain death.

Now he was directly over the northern rampart, sailing down its length. It rose toward him. Bolan was landing like an airplane, at an angle to the tower. He was going to crash into it. Bolan pulled on both toggles at once, arresting his forward movement. He came straight down, a little too high but it beat the hell out of smashing into the tower. The jump boots smacked the stone, shock waves traveled through his teeth, but he landed standing.

The canopy sailed over the side. Before it had time to drag him down, he punched the release buckle. In a flash he was out of the harness and running for the tower, unslinging the Sterling from across his back. He knew the guard had heard the sound of the landing.

The arc light in the tower shifted to the rampart, blinding him. He dropped to a knee as the sound-suppressed Sterling uttered its muted chatter. The light went out with a crash of shattered glass, and Bolan sprinted for the tower. The guard swung the machine gun at him, but he was past the angle of fire.

Bolan reached for the handle of the door leading to the tower. The key grated in the lock, the soldier inside beating him to it. Bolan unhooked a smoke grenade from his gun belt, primed it and pushed it through a slit in the tower. He heard it fall and swish with smoke. The soldier began coughing, then let out a cry.

The key grated in the lock again and Bolan stood back, the Sterling on his hip. The door opened and the soldier appeared wheezing and coughing, surrounded by swirling smoke. The Sterling stuttered and the man toppled forward.

A burst of gunfire resounded from the parade ground. There were shouts as a grenade exploded. A few more bursts, then all hell broke loose. On the rampart, the light from the northwest tower went out. The former legionnaire had done his job. The fort's siren began wailing.

Bolan sprinted along the parapet toward the door that led inside the fort. It was padlocked. He raised the muzzle of his gun and fired, shattering the lock. With a well-placed kick he had the door open. He raced inside and came to a dimly lit corridor. Soldiers were running toward him, obviously heading for the stairwell that led to the ramparts. He crouched and squeezed the trigger, peppering the corridor with slugs. There were screams of agony as the projectiles found their mark.

Bolan jumped back into the stairwell. The survivors were returning fire. He primed a smoke grenade and, with a quick in and out, sent it rolling on the floor toward the soldiers. It exploded as he pulled on his oxygen mask and goggles. He changed magazines and came out firing, hitting two soldiers who were creeping toward him. He ran into the patch of smoke.

As he came out, he saw the other enemies bunched up, waiting to charge as soon as the smoke cleared. At the sight of Bolan there were shouts and shots. Bolan dived back into the smoke. He crouched, primed a fragmentation grenade and lobbed it. An ear-splitting explosion rocked the corridor, the confinement amplifying the sound, followed by screams of pain. Bolan came out of the smoke, his weapon blazing. Before the survivors had time to react he was running along another corridor.

The fort shook from explosions. A moment later bugles sounded outside the wall. Bolan turned and ran, his thick-soled jump boots moving quietly on the stone floor. He came to the communications room, took off the mask and goggles and listened by the slightly opened door. A voice was shouting in Vietnamese.

He also heard the tapping sound of a Morse key in action.

Bolan nudged the door with his foot, and it swung open to reveal two men in pajamas. One was sitting by the Morse transmitter with his earphones on, the second stood a few feet away by a voice set. The one shouting was the first to die. The second never knew what hit him.

The room fell still. Outside, the fighting was picking up,

the gunfire drowning out the wailing siren. Bolan could hear the Vietnamese AK-47s dueling with the Khmer Rouge M-16s. The sound of so many M-16s told him the assault force was inside the fort. A grenade explosion sent tremors through the building.

Bolan locked the door. He crossed the room to the voice set and brought the receiver to his ear. It hissed with static, but nothing else.

One of the windows in the room shattered. A hole appeared in a curtain and in the ceiling. The outside noise filled the room. Bolan adjusted the dial to the desired frequency.

"Nighthawk to Speedbird," he said.

"Speedbird."

"We're inside," Bolan said.

"Coming," replied the CIA hovercraft pilot.

Bolan raised his weapon to shoot at the radio set, then changed his mind. Might need it, he thought. He opened the door and eased himself out onto the corridor, locking the door behind him.

The building was deserted; everyone was outside fighting. He crossed several corridors and came to a locked door. He rapped on it and pointed the muzzle at the little slide door at head height. When the slide opened, Bolan fired.

The guard toppled back. Bolan shot the lock and kicked the door open. An AK-47 spat flame. Bolan stepped aside, then entered the doorway firing. A second guard died.

Bolan came to the door of the American dormitory. He kicked it open and entered.

On the wall poster, Uncle Sam pointed his finger at him as usual. Men in striped pajamas looked at him from the beds. But half the beds were empty.

13

The rescue force rolled toward the uranium mine.

In the turret of the armored car, Bolan primed the machine gun.

Behind him were four trucks carrying Khmer Rouge and POWs—the prisoners from the fort.

The other prisoners had been in the mine working the newly instituted night shift. Now they were being held hostage. Their captors were garrison soldiers who had barricaded themselves in the tunnel leading to the mine.

"All commanders," Bolan said into his walkie-talkie. "Remember to stick to your targets. P'um's group attacks the ground installations, Cosgrove's men go down to take the barricade in the rear. My men will find and rescue the prisoners."

"Roger," Cosgrove said.

"Understood," P'um said.

In his earphones Bolan heard the car driver mutter. "Lucky for us this armored car was spending the night at the fort."

Damn lucky, he thought. Without the car's cannon they could not storm the mine.

The convoy went over the hill, and the illuminated mine came into view. Everything looked normal.

"Maybe we'll surprise them," the driver said.

"I doubt it," Bolan replied.

They did not. As the convoy turned off the coastal road onto the strip leading to the gates, arc lights came on and tracers flew at them from machine guns on the miradors. From inside the compound came pops. Mortar bombs exploded around them.

"Disperse," Bolan shouted into the walkie-talkie. The trucks drove off the road into the trees. He slid into the turret, closing the hatch cover over him.

The armored car continued toward the gate, its eight wheels kicking up a cloud of dust. Colored tracers bounced off its thick shell.

In the turret, eyes glued to the periscope, Bolan aimed the cannon at the gate. He pressed the firing pedal and the cannon roared, blowing away half the gate. He fired again and the way was clear.

They bumped over the debris and rolled into the compound. Bolan swiveled the turret 360 degrees, the cannon barrel rising as far as it would go. The platform of the first mirador came into the gunsight.

Bolan ordered the driver to stop.

The vehicle screeched to a halt and Bolan pressed the pedal again. The tower disintegrated as if in slow motion, hurling a body through the air. He swiveled the gun onto the next mirador. It, too, crashed amid dust and flame.

"Go!" Bolan commanded.

The Rhino rolled, the turret tracking back to face forward. They drove toward the center of the compound, heading for the mortar emplacement.

The emplacement came into view and Bolan activated the cannon. The area flashed with explosions that tossed disintegrating sandbags all over the compound. There was a bright flare as a shell hit a stack of bombs, taking out the mortar battery. Bolan emerged from the hatch and finished off the survivors with the machine gun.

Atop the water tower, a siren began wailing.

"Go trucks. Go trucks!" Bolan shouted into the walkie-talkie.

"Where to now?" the driver asked.

"Let's take a tour," Bolan replied.

They drove around, Bolan shooting up everything in sight, keeping the enemy off balance, making way for the arrival of the trucks.

The trucks came a few minutes later, muzzles spitting flame from the open backs, fanning out for their respective targets.

Bolan's walkie-talkie blared. "Minehead secured."

"Drive to the shaft," Bolan ordered the driver.

They pulled up outside the shed that housed the mine shaft. Bolan leaped to the ground and entered the hut. The place was busy with POWs. Men were shouting orders. Winching machinery whined and the cage was going down, taking men to the first-level tunnel for the attack on the barricades. On the ground lay the bodies of three Vietnamese soldiers who had been guarding the shed.

"Sir." It was Romero, a third-generation Mexican American, and Bolan's second-in-command, calling him to a table on which was spread a map of the mine. "They're holding the prisoners in the winze room on the eighth level." He pointed to the spot on the map.

Within minutes Bolan's group entered the cage. Ten men. The gate shut, a bell rang and the hoist machinery whined. The cage descended into a dark, silent world. There was no light in either the cage or the shaft. The only lights they saw flickered as the station levels flashed by.

When they passed the sixth level, the cage began slowing

down. Bolan opened the door while the cage was still moving, and the others stood to the side. Bolan stood in the middle, his silenced Sterling on his hip. Light appeared and the cage came to a halt on the seventh-level station.

In front of Bolan was a small rocky room lit by a solitary forty-watt bulb with a metal shade. At the far end was the entrance to a tunnel. A Vietnamese soldier was sitting on the ground, his rifle leaning against a wall. He saw Bolan, but moved too late for his weapon. Bolan's Sterling chattered.

The soldier grunted, the rifle clattering to the ground. Bolan entered the room. The men remained in the cage. He stopped to listen. The place was hot and humid, the silence oppressive. Only the sound of dripping water disturbed the stillness. Bolan brought out a torch and poked it into the tunnel high above his head. Empty.

He went around the back, his jump boots making no sound. He passed a line of empty cars standing on rails and entered another rocky room. This one contained machinery for pumping water out of the mine.

"Is that you, Fa?" someone asked from a side cave. Light came from there.

Bolan walked over and looked in. Two soldiers were playing dice by the light of a candle. The Sterling hissed twice and two more bodies toppled over. Bolan returned to the level station.

"Okay, the coast is clear," he whispered.

They made their way into the tunnel, torches bobbing, their footsteps echoing eerily, the torches illuminating wet black walls and timber roof beams. It was a good half kilometer to the winze room, and until the last hundred meters, they did not need to worry about noise.

They were halfway there when they were challenged.

"Password!" When no reply came, the Vietnamese opened fire. Tracers flew through the dark, bouncing off walls.

"So much for the operator's information," said Bolan, hugging the ground. "He said no guards in the tunnel."

Bolan's mind whirled. They had to find some way of getting past these soldiers. To crawl up to them would take too long, and chances of getting to them alive were minimal. As for smoke grenades, he could not lob that far, not with such a low tunnel roof.

"The cars," he said. "How are they propelled?"

"Some have electric engines," Romero said. "They push the others."

"Okay, pull back," Bolan instructed.

As soon as they began crawling, the enemy heard them and started shooting. Eventually they managed to reach a curve in the tunnel. They stood up and ran. They reached the level station, started an engine car and piled into the train. They rumbled toward the winze room, the cavelike room that served as an intersection for the passageways that connected each level.

As the train rounded the bend, the Vietnamese guards opened fire. Bullets clanged against the lead car but the train kept going, Bolan and Romero shooting over the side, the others crouching low inside their cars.

The guards turned to run. At that moment, Romero lit the headlight of the lead car. They could see the backs of six soldiers running down the side of the tracks. Bolan and Romero mowed them down.

Light appeared at the end of the tunnel. Everyone jumped out and began running behind the train. Bolan moved from the front car into the second. He put on his goggles and his oxygen mask. He primed two smoke grenades and threw one in the head car, one into the car behind him. In no time, he was engulfed in swirling smoke.

The train rumbled into the room where the Americans were held. The astounded Vietnamese guards stood watching, unable to figure out what was going on in the smoky haze. Bolan squeezed the Sterling's trigger, his first target the machine-gun crew. He fired burst after burst, killing guards as the train passed.

The train left the room, bullets pinging off the side of the cars as the surviving guards fired at Bolan. They made an easy target for Bolan's team, who shot them all. The action was over in seconds.

Bolan jumped out of the train, leaving it to roll on. He ran back into the room, taking his mask off. He looked around and saw the prisoners huddled in a far corner, exactly as Romero had indicated. "Everyone to the level station. There's a boat coming to pick us up," he shouted.

The startled Americans jogged down the tunnel, lights bobbing—men hungry for freedom.

Bolan and Romero brought up the rear.

"The CIA wants us to destroy the mine," Bolan told him.

"It won't be too difficult," Romero said. "A couple of grenades against the pumps will start the flooding process. Then we blow up the cage inside the shaft. It would take a year to reopen the mine."

"Let's do it," Bolan said.

They came to the level station and called for the cage. While the men were evacuated, Bolan and Romero destroyed the pumps. Next they went to the first level, to a cave where explosives were stored. By then the battle in the tunnel was over. The enemy had surrendered when caught in the crossfire. On the surface, the fighting was also over.

When everyone was out of the mine, they loaded the cage with explosives and sent it down the shaft between the first and second levels. Bolan waited by the armored car for the charge to go off. He had primed it with a twenty-minute fuse.

A tremor shook the ground. It was done. Bolan climbed into the car. "Let's go."

They drove past smoking ruins, bodies, a howling dog looking for its master. The sky grew light. It was dawn.

"Pretty quick work," the driver said. In less than an hour, they had destroyed the mine, forced the remnants of the garrison to surrender and rescued the POWs. "Very neat."

"Too neat," Bolan said. He had the superstitious feeling that things were going too well.

He got back to the fort and received the news.

The CIA hovercraft had broken down.

Now they'd have to make their own way out of the country.

He knew the breaks wouldn't last.

14

Through the window of the camp commandant's office, Bolan gazed down onto the parade ground where hundreds of black-clad guerrillas squatted around campfires cooking breakfast. The morning was gray and windy. From the flagpole fluttered flags that showed three yellow towers on a red background. The fort's walls were covered with graffiti glorifying the forces of liberation. Between the guerrillas, carrying wood and water for cooking, moved a new set of POWs, Vietnamese.

"You don't have to do this," Bolan said. "The others can guide us just as well."

"I know I don't," Eng said from her chair. "But I want to."

"It will be dangerous."

"No more than bringing you into the country."

"Yes, it will. No one was looking for us then. This time there will be a dragnet. We may never get out."

There was a knock on the door. "I will be in the communications room." She left through a side door.

"Come in," Bolan called.

Cosgrove and Romero entered, side arms strapped to their brown prison overalls. "You sent for us," Cosgrove said.

"Take a seat," Bolan said, motioning them to chairs facing Colonel Minh's desk. He sat down behind it.

"I've got news," he said. "The CIA is not coming."

"We heard," Cosgrove replied.

"So we're on our own."

"When you say 'we,' exactly who do you mean?" Romero asked.

"I mean the American POWs," Bolan replied. "My mission is to rescue the Americans, not the other nationalities."

"I am afraid we can't agree to that," Cosgrove said. "Either we all leave or no one goes."

"Is that a personal opinion?"

"I am giving you the unanimous opinion of the American contingent. Having been sold out ourselves, we're not going to start selling out others."

"I see," Bolan said. He felt a weight off his shoulders. From the start of the mission he had pushed for having all nationalities included in the rescue. But both the League and the CIA had turned down the idea. Now Cosgrove had handed him his freedom to act.

"Agreed," Bolan said. "Everyone is to be included in the escape. What I propose is this: we drive inland, then head for the Thai border either on foot or in the trucks using trails. The Khmer Rouge will provide us with guides. You in agreement?"

The two POWs exchanged looks. "Sir, the opinion of the camp is that we should head for Laos," Romero said.

"Laos?"

"There's another POW camp in southern Laos, near Pakse," Cosgrove said. "It's a tobacco estate near the Mekong. There are one hundred five prisoners, including twenty-four Americans. Like us, they are being held for ransom."

"We know this from two new arrivals," interjected

Romero. "They came to the fort last week to work the mine. They're from Laos."

It was madness, Pakse was a good six hundred kilometers away. And yet .... Bolan deeply shared the attitude of the two men before him. Rather than grab their freedom and run, these men were going to risk it to bring freedom to others.

"Sir?" Romero said. "The camp will understand if you do not wish to come along. You have done so much for us already. But if you will not come, we would appreciate the use of your guides."

Bolan toyed absently with a pencil. "You realize, of course, that if we do march into Laos, the CIA will wash their hands of us. I mean, completely. Right now they might still be persuaded to bail us out if we got into a jam."

"We're already in a jam, sir," Romero said.

As if to underline his point, the fort's siren began to wail. Then there was the sound of running feet in the corridor. P'um burst into the room.

"The Vietnamese," he panted. "A whole regiment."

FROM THE RAMPARTS, Bolan observed the enemy through field glasses. Soldiers milled on the access road to the fort beside a long line of trucks. He could hear whistles and orders being shouted as the men loaded up with equipment and formed into units. They were mountain troops, he could tell by their burgundy berets. The soldiers carried rope ladders and grappling hooks and mortar to fire them.

"They're going to scale the walls," Bolan said.

"Let them," said Baday, the commander of the proletarian brigade who was standing next to him. "We'll give them hell."

The heaviest armament the enemy had was machine

guns. Aside from the small tubes for firing hooks, Bolan could not see anything else they could use to bombard the fort. He guessed they did not want to burn it down; a mortar bombardment would start fires.

"Looks as if they want to take the fort back intact," he said.

"And of course they think they can do it," Baday replied. "To them we are simply disorganized bandits."

They watched the troops move out. One group headed for the woods that faced the northern wall, another for the trees to the south.

Bolan spoke into his walkie-talkie. "All commanders, the enemy is planning to scale the walls. A simultaneous assault from north and south. Cosgrove?"

"Here," the other replied.

"I'll need your men on the ramparts with instruments for prying grappling hooks. There should be lots of them in the armory and garage. Also, try the maintenance room and the gym. But do it fast. P'um?"

"Sir."

"Assemble the tower machine gunners by the northeastern tower. I want to have a chat with them."

The walkie-talkie again came to life. "Communications room to Nighthawk."

"Yes," Bolan responded.

"We are going to be attacked from the air," Eng said. "We cannot understand everything—they are using code—but the Yen Sai operator is referring to T-28s. Do you know the plane?"

"Yes," Bolan said. It was a prop-driven trainer of World War II vintage, which the U.S. reactivated for anti-guerrilla operations in the Vietnam War. Now, the Vietnamese were using them. "Any indication of the numbers?"

"Four," Eng replied.

"Thanks, White Lotus." Bolan tapped the talk button twice. "Got that Romero?"

"Copied."

"I want you to organize an air defense," Bolan said. "There are some Brownings with water coolers in the armory. I saw tripods, too. We'll need them on the ramparts."

"What about crews? I'd be more comfortable with our men."

Bolan glanced at Baday, but the Khmer Rouge general had moved off and was out of earshot. "Watch that, Romero, or we'll have a diplomatic incident." Already the Khmer Rouge had complained that too many top posts were going to the POWs.

"Locals, then," Romero said.

Bolan nodded.

He put the walkie-talkie on his shoulder and leaned over the northern rampart. The woods below were crawling with enemy soldiers. On the edge, men were digging machine gun emplacements. Bolan was tempted to fire on them, but dismissed the thought. If his group started shooting, the enemy would give up the idea of scaling the walls and decide on an artillery or air bombardment. And that would spell certain doom for the defenders.

Bolan reached for the walkie-talkie again.

"Romero?"

"I read you."

"I want you to range your mortar on the edge of the woods, half the tubes on the northern wood, half on the south. They are setting up machine guns. Pound that area as soon as the siren sounds. After you've taken out the guns, cease fire and conserve your bombs until you hear from me. Got that?"

"Got it."

The walkie-talkie blared. "Godor to Nighthawk. Floor one. North, ready for inspection."

Bolan descended a stairway to the corridor below. Two hundred guerrillas stood with automatic rifles. There were also four machine guns. As Bolan walked past them with Godor, the corridor commander, he realized something was missing. Grenades. He turned to Godor.

"Go to the armory and bring up ten cases of grenades. Distribute them among your men and tell them they are not to use them until I give the word. Radio the commander of Floor one, South, and tell him to do the same."

Godor started shouting orders.

Bolan climbed the stairwell back to the ramparts. The tower gunners were assembled and waiting for him. All four had stars on their sleeves, identifying them as marksmen. They were older men, the operation of the tower guns requiring responsibility and experience. Bolan explained to them how the enemy was going to launch the attack, then told them what their targets would be.

"As soon as the siren sounds, you will open fire on the machine guns in the woods. As soon as the enemy begins climbing the walls, I want you to forget about those guns. Others will be shooting at them. Train your guns on the men climbing the walls."

The gunners trotted off, and Bolan began positioning the AA machine guns, which had arrived along with men carrying sandbags to build emplacements for them. There were only three guns, and he had counted five in the armory. He radioed Romero and found out that the others did not have water coolers, so Romero was using them for ground fire. The coolers were needed for sustained fire.

He was almost finished positioning the guns when the

door of a stairwell opened and POWs emerged, rifles on their backs, carrying all sorts of prying equipment. It looked as if the fort had been stripped of every bit of metal that could serve as a lever. The men held bars, poles and spikes, long wrenches and pliers, jimmies, beams, tubes, metal table legs; one man even carried a weight-lifting bar. To Bolan the POWs looked like factory workers taking part in a revolution. He saw a special look in their eyes, the look of men determined to go down fighting. Not one of them would surrender. Bolan was sure of that. They had done it once and paid for it with years of slavery.

Bolan addressed them.

"The enemy is treating this battle as a training exercise, to see how their troops would fare scaling under fire. That's what happens when people are in power for too long: they get overconfident and start making mistakes. We must exploit this.

"Remember, the ramparts will be swept by concentrated machine-gun fire, at least at the beginning of the assault. Keep your heads down. When you pry hooks from the crenels, stay behind the merlons. Your main task is not to shoot at the enemy, that is the task of the men on the floors below you. Your job is to prevent the enemy from gaining a foothold on the ramparts."

The men moved off to take positions. Bolan racked his brain for something he might have forgotten. From experience, he knew that battles were not won by bravery, but by organization. Then he remembered.

"Nighthawk to Hippo."

"Hippo," replied the doctor-parachutist.

"How's it coming?"

"The last sandbag is going up," the doctor replied. He

was in charge of sandbagging the side gates, which had been blown the night before.

"As soon as you're through, get to your post," Bolan said. He had organized a field hospital in the fort's basement.

"Aircraft!" shouted a voice on the ramparts.

In the sky over the sea four dots were approaching. As they drew closer, Bolan recognized them as T-28s. The men on the ramparts raised their rifles, the AA gunners swiveled their guns. The planes grew larger, the sky filling with the sound of their engines. Bolan saw lights wink on the wings as bullets swept the rooftops of the fort.

On the ramparts, an AA machine gun opened up and everyone joined in. The noise was deafening. Over the din, Bolan could hear all three Brownings firing in bursts.

The planes roared over, leaving bodies in their wake. Bolan cursed himself for not following Romero's suggestion to let POWs man the guns. The Khmer Rouge crews did not know anything about handling AA guns. Firing in bursts! He sprinted for the machine gun nearest to him and pushed the gunner aside. To hell with diplomacy.

The T-28s were making a second pass. Bolan aimed the gun ahead of the leading plane, squeezed the trigger and held it there, letting the plane fly into the tracers. He sent out a continuous line of fire.

The leading T-28 flew through Bolan's tracers with no damage, and now its wing flickered as it opened fire. Geysers slashed across the rooftops. But Bolan ignored them, his attention on the next plane. The other machine guns joined in so that three lines of tracers converged on the spot ahead of the second T-28.

The crisscrossing tracers started to riddle the plane. The second T-28 banked, smoke pouring from its engine. The pilot made a wide turn back out to sea, the stricken aircraft losing height all the time. Finally a wing tip caught the water and the aircraft tumbled tail over nose, and disappeared into the ocean.

The last two planes roared overhead. They joined up with the first one and came around for the next pass. Once again three lines of colored gun tracers marked the sky. They crisscrossed ahead of the lead plane, and the gun crews waited for it to fly into the tracers. Seeing this, the pilot banked, but the crisscross swung with him, zeroing in on its exposed belly. Struck, the plane rolled and went into a downward spin.

The remaining aircraft broke formation and flew away.

A cheer arose from the men on the ramparts.

They had beaten off the air attack. Faces were flushed with victory as they awaited the enemy's next move.

The sound of bugles came from the woods. *"Quanca!"* The countryside echoed with the Vietnamese battle cry as soldiers poured from behind the trees carrying ladders, mortar and grappling hooks. The fort's siren began wailing, and the defenders opened up their counter attack.

"Begin firing," Bolan shouted over the din into the walkie-talkie.

Joining the noise of the siren, mortars banged. A half-dozen bombs rose into the sky. Bolan watched the northern woods flash with exploding shells. A fountain of earth and flame rose from a machine-gun emplacement on the edge of the woods. Gun and bodies were hurled into the air.

The next moment Bolan heard a man scream over the noise of the shouting. In front of him a POW was running around wildly, hands over his face, blood streaming through his fingers. Bolan sprinted to help him. Before he could reach him, an enemy machine gun swept the ramparts. The POW's head exploded and he fell over the side.

Enemy mortar fired below. Everywhere grappling hooks clanged on stone. Two hooks caught on embrasures flanking the northeastern tower. Neither embrasure had a defender; the men manning them were dead.

Bolan grabbed one of their bars and ran to the nearest hook. He dug the bar under a prong, levering it up until he freed the hook from the top. It grated and fell off.

Bolan ran to the other side of the tower and began working on the next hook. But it did not budge. He leaned over the side and saw two men climbing the rope. The double weight held the hook tightly against the wall.

Bolan dropped the bar and whipped out a knife. He leaned over and began sawing at the rope. Bullets smacked the walls about him, but he ignored them. The lead soldier looked up and saw Bolan hacking at the hemp. Frantically the man started climbing faster and as he came within an arm's length of Bolan, he pulled out his own knife. Twining the rope around his leg to avoid slipping, and clutching his support with one hand, he slashed at Bolan with the blade.

Bolan jumped clear of the swipe and the knife scraped the wall. He leaned out and resumed cutting. The soldier regained his balance and made another thrust. Again Bolan pulled back. While the soldier regained his balance he cut the rope a little more.

The soldier kept slashing, Bolan kept cutting, the two men oblivious to the shouting· and the gunfire around them. The soldier began tiring, his slashes became less frequent and less energetic. It was exhausting just to stay up because he was weighted with a rifle and ammunition pouches.

Bit by bit Bolan's cuts went deeper. There was a shearing noise as several strands gave way. The soldier made one last attempt to get Bolan. He pulled himself up with all his might, aiming the knife at Bolan's face. But the pull also put an extra strain on the rope, and the last strands snapped. The two soldiers fell screaming to earth, sprawling as they hit the ground.

Bolan heard a clang as another grappling hook caught a nearby opening. He grabbed it and pulled it toward himself before the man below had time to put his weight on it. He threw the hook over the side, then looked about him. Everywhere there was hand-to-hand fighting.

The enemy had gained a foothold on the ramparts, helped by the overheated tower machine guns, which were now silent. Here and there a shot rang out. But there were mainly shouts, grunts and the thud of metal against metal or bone. A frenzy seemed to have taken hold of attackers and defenders alike, each side clubbing at one another.

Bolan peered over the rampart. A mass of burgundy berets was milling around the base of the wall as the enemy waited to climb the ladders and ropes. The soldiers were in no immediate danger of being fired upon—the tower guns were jammed, and the gunmen on the floor below could not aim their weapons that low.

"Floors one, North and South," Bolan shouted into his walkie-talkie, "start throwing grenades."

Grenades rained on the enemy but the principal effect was nil—the Khmer Rouge were dropping them immediately after priming, not knowing that the grenades had four-second fuses. The enemy soldiers were able to throw the grenades away before they exploded.

"All commanders," Bolan shouted into his radio, "tell your men to count to two before throwing grenades."

Even as he shouted, he knew it was a waste of breath. The middle of a battle is not the time to start training troops. Bolan looked about and saw the AA machine gun on the western rampart, abandoned by its crew, which had gone to fight the climbing attackers.

Bolan dashed into the northeastern tower. He shouted to the gunner and his assistant to bring the AA gun. Then he radioed Cosgrove to do the same thing with the two guns at his end. Then he moved out the jammed gun. The two men returned with the AA gun, Bolan installed it and opened fire.

With the cooler on, he was able to pour sustained fire into the mass of men below. They began going down like pins in a bowling alley. Then a second AA gun opened from the tower on the other end of the wall and the massacre began.

From the woods bugles sounded the retreat. The enemy soldiers climbing the ropes slid to the ground, those on the ramparts broke off and went over the side after them. Bolan reached for his walkie-talkie.

"Romero, open fire."

Mortar bombs swooshed out of the sky, exploding among the retreating troops. At the same time, the fire from the arrow slits in the walls increased now that there were targets again. Lines of men fell before reaching the woods.

"Cease fire!" Bolan shouted.

Gunfire died. Silence settled over the ramparts. Everywhere there were bodies. The exhausted defenders leaned against the merlons, or slid to the ground. There was a profusion of bleeding faces and wounded arms and legs.

Cosgrove came up to Bolan. "We did it."

"Yeah," said Bolan wearily.

As he lit a cigarette the walkie-talkie blared.

"Nighthawk," Bolan replied.

"We have intercepted a message from the commander of the regiment," Eng said. "He reports forty percent casualties. He has asked permission to withdraw. Wait." There was a long pause. "Yen Sai has answered him. They have told him to launch another attack tonight. They are sending him a battalion of mountain troops as reinforcement. And they are sending a tank. That is all."

"Why a tank?" Cosgrove asked.

"For the gate, I suspect," Bolan said.

"We've got to break out before those reinforcements get here," Cosgrove said.

"Not in daylight," Bolan said, shaking his head. "There's still sixty percent of that regiment out there."

"We beat them once, we can do it again," Cosgrove said.

"We beat them because they had walls to climb. On the ground it will be a different story. We'll wait until dark."

"You have a plan?" Cosgrove asked.

Bolan nodded. A lie, but there was no sense in discouraging the men. "I'll be in the communications room," he said, rising. Once more he was faced with the task of saving lives by military means, by tactic and strategy and the spilling of blood. Once more he would have to stretch his combat mind to the very limit to devise a method to defend, kill, save. Once more he would put his life on the line—his life of deadly commitment and terrible bereavement—in order that others might preserve their lives and grow in dignity.

Once more he would identify...infiltrate...destroy!

THE SPOTTER PLANE circled in the sky. Bolan and Eng watched it from the western rampart as they ate lunch.

"Have you thought of how we are going to get out of here?" she asked.

"Not yet," he replied.

"You'll think of something," Eng said.

"Here comes the mortar man."

It was Romero. He bowed to Eng and spoke to Bolan. "Taking a tour of forbidden areas. Can you imagine? Five years I lived here and never once set foot on these ramparts. They were out of bounds, together with the corridors leading to the side gates. May I join you?"

They made room for him and he sat down.

Romero looked up at the circling plane. "I wonder what he's up to?"

"Keeping an eye on us, I imagine," Bolan said. "In case we try a breakout."

"Cosgrove said you decided to wait until dark," Romero went on.

"Yes," Bolan said.

"I agree. In daylight we wouldn't stand a chance."

"Are there explosives in the mine?" Bolan asked.

"Explosives?" Romero repeated. "There's enough explosive down there to blow up half of Yen Sai. That room I took you to is only one of the storage areas. Funny thing, we were always short of things—spare parts, lubricants, acids—but never explosives."

Bolan remained silent. Then it hit him.

Enough explosives to blow up half of Yen Sai. . . .

15

The tank lumbered toward the fort, treads clattering in the night. The murmur of several hundred men walking in its wake could be heard over its rumblings. The time was 2100 hours and the second assault on the fort was under way. A dozen POWs waited behind machine guns on the rampart above the main gate. Twenty more were inside the fort. Together they represented the sum of Bolan's defenses— the rest of the garrison was sitting out the battle in the tunnel to the mine.

"Activate the siren," Bolan ordered into his walkie-talkie.

The siren wailed and the gunners on the rampart opened fire.

Tracers flew down at the approaching enemy, those aimed at the tank bouncing harmlessly off its metal exterior.

The marching men scattered into the bordering woods to continue their advance under cover of the trees. On the edge of the tree line, enemy machine guns opened up in reply.

The armored vehicle, a slow moving beetle, rolled alone on the access road.

"Mortar battery, commence firing," Bolan said into his radio.

A firestorm erupted from the parade ground, and the

woods lit up with widely spread flashes. They did not impede the enemy's advance—they were too far apart—but that was not their purpose. Like the machine-gun fire, the mortar fire was mainly for show, a lot of noise to give the enemy the impression the defenders were fighting back.

The machine guns blasted away, sixteen of them manned by twelve men. The guns had attachments to hold triggers in firing positions, the gunners merely aiming them in different directions from time to time to add realism. In this way, the POWs did not expose themselves to the bullets sweeping the ramparts from the enemy's guns in the woods.

The tank entered the clearing in front of the fort. Bolan recognized the combat vehicle as a T-62, an ancient model. But its armor was thick enough to protect it from the mortar shells and machine-gun fire.

The turret swiveled as the commander brought the 85mm cannon on target. A tongue of flame left the muzzle and the fort shook on impact. The main gate crashed to the ground amid a cloud of dust. Bugles sounded and with a battle cry the attackers ran out from the woods. By the light of the moon, Bolan could see they no longer wore berets; this time they had helmets.

The POWs pulled away from the guns, leaving some to fire on their own, and ran along the northern rampart for the back of the fort to join those already in the tunnel. Only Bolan remained. He stood by the flagpole and watched the enemy stream into the fort.

One group surged down the main alley leading to the parade ground, another fanned into bordering buildings to make a parallel advance along the corridors. The enemy's battle plan was to flush out the guerrillas using speed and superior training.

From rooftops and windows came flashes as the other POWs began playing their part. Corridors erupted with grenade explosions. None of it was enough to stop the enemy, but it was enough to give them the idea the defenders were trying.

Satisfied everything was going according to plan, Bolan dropped to one knee and emptied a magazine on the mass of men below.

At all cost the enemy must not be given time to think, to consider why there were not more people shooting at them, why their progress could be so rapid.

Bolan moved away from his position, slid down a rope and ran toward a sandbag bunker next to the mortar battery. It was freshly built and had an observation slit in the side facing the fort. Cosgrove stood inside, smoking in the dark.

"Ready?" Bolan said.

"Anytime," Cosgrove replied.

They saw men emerging from doors, some carrying their wounded. They were the inside POW teams. They ran across the parade ground away from the approaching shouts and explosions, and disappeared into a stairwell that led down to the tunnel.

"How many more?" Bolan shouted as he stepped out of the bunker.

"One team," Romero said.

A door opened and three men ran out. They were instantly cut down by a burst of AK-47 fire. The enemy units had reached the parade ground.

"Everyone into the tunnel," Bolan ordered.

The mortar crews ran for the stairwell as more gunfire sent tracers toward the mortar battery and the bunker. Bolan ducked, running for the bunker.

"Everyone gone?" Cosgrove called out. He flicked the cigarette butt away, the red glow arcing into the night. For him, the upcoming event was as routine as blowing up rock in a mine.

"Do it," Bolan said.

Cosgrove clicked a switch and an earthquakelike tremor rumbled through the ground as the fort began to collapse. It was completely different from what Bolan had expected. He had imagined there would be a booming explosion with flaming debris flying into the air. Instead there was a continuous rumble as building after building imploded, the walls cracking and falling down, the roofs caving in. The only thing that went up was dust—tons of it.

The rumbling ended and a deathly silence settled over the ruins. Bolan stood as if transfixed. One moment an impressive fort, the next so much rubble. And under the wreckage were several hundred men, their lives snuffed out.

"Attack," he shouted into his walkie-talkie.

The defenders emerged from the stairwell, splitting into two groups, one heading for the side gate in the northern wall of the parade ground, the other toward the southern wall. The remnants of the enemy would be taken in a pincer movement. Not all the enemy troops had been killed. There were still the machine-gun crews and the reserve units in the woods. Bolan knew this because Eng had overheard the Vietnamese commander describe his battle plan on the radio to Yen Sai.

A group led by Bolan and P'um made its way along the northern wall, parts of which had collapsed. A strong breeze was blowing away the dust, and the wall was once again bathed in moonlight. The ruins presented an eerie spectacle: stark and desolate, and hushed.

Then gunfire.

Everyone hit the ground. Bolan reached for his walkie-talkie. "Enemy machine guns in the northeastern wood!"

A mortar banged and bombs swooshed out of the sky. Fountains of white phosphorous lit the woods. Trees and vegetation caught fire. Screams pierced the air.

The enemy ran off as more bombs swooshed down.

"Forward!" Bolan shouted and the guerrillas charged.

They were almost at the northeast corner when Bolan heard an exhaust backfire. The tank. Cold sweat broke out on his forehead. The tank had survived destruction. Now it might block their escape. He handed P'um the walkie-talkie. "Take over," he shouted and ran ahead.

Bolan rounded the corner and saw the tank emerging from the gaping hole that had been the gate; now a fast-moving beetle. The operator turned on a single headlamp and the machine clattered away, retreating down the access road toward the coastal highway. Bolan sprinted after it.

The armored vehicle passed some burning trucks, then a long line of undamaged trucks and jeeps. Bolan and the POWs needed the vehicles to make their getaway, but now they were threatened by the lumbering shape ahead.

The tank changed gears and picked up speed. Bolan kept running, anger lending him extra force.

The tank slowed down to negotiate a turn on the coastal road. Bolan cut across a field, arriving at the road as the tank was about to pass. The driver must have seen him because the machine suddenly swung onto the shoulder to run him down. Bolan jumped out of the way, then sprinted up a low rise in the terrain. Just before the tank changed gears again, he leaped onto it. He still had his Sterling and a couple of fragmentation grenades.

Bolan made his way to the turret, searching for the

hatches. He would drop a grenade inside. The commander's hatch was locked. He worked his way to the front, looking for the driver's and gunner's hatches. There weren't any—the Vietnamese-made version of the T-62 had only one hatch.

The slits. He would slip a grenade through an opening. He looked into the nearest one. A shout of surprise greeted him, and the tank picked up speed, making the ride even bumpier. They were trying to shake him off. The commander's slit had bars, too narrow for a grenade. He checked the gunner's and the driver's opening. Also too narrow.

The exhaust pipe. Bolan worked his way to the back. A grating covered the pipe. Despair seized him. He was astride the tank but he was powerless. Then he saw the bobbing cannon in front.

He decided he'd push a grenade down the barrel. When the grenade reached the chamber, it would detonate the shell in it. The tank would go sky high, and with a four- second fuse he'd have time to jump off. Trouble was, the cannon's barrel ran parallel to the ground. The grenade might fall out from the bumping. Still, he must try.

First he decided to secure his rear position. While he was on the barrel, the commander might pop up from his hatch and simply shoot him with a pistol. He'd have to block the hatch.

He crawled to the turret to examine the hatch. On either side were handles. It should be a simple matter to block it by sticking something over the hatch and under the handles.

But there were no tools attached to the tank.

Then he remembered the Sterling.

Bolan took off his gun and measured it against the hatch. Perfect. He unclipped the sling, inserted the gun under the handles, passed the sling over them and clipped it back on. The gun stayed securely in place.

Bolan made his way to the front of the tank. He wrapped himself around the barrel and pulled himself along it with his hands and legs, lying on top of it.

Behind him he could hear the commander pounding on the blocked hatch.

Bolan ignored the sound, concentrating on his progress. The muzzle came nearer. Suddenly he felt himself moving sideways, the turret swiveling to the right. Then it jerked to the left, then right again. He hung on. It was a tough job to prevent himself from slipping under the barrel, and slip he did. For a hair-raising moment, he hung from the barrel by his hands, the ground rushing under his feet, the clattering treads ready to pulverize him if he fell. He swung back and forth, giving himself momentum. On the third swing forward he was able to bring his legs up all the way and wrap them around the barrel.

The tank left the road, heading for the woods. They were going to scrape him off. Bolan tightened his leg grip on the barrel and with one hand reached for a grenade from his belt. He brought himself up so that he hung by the crook of an arm. He pulled the safety pin but kept the spoon on safety.

The woods neared. It would be touch and go.

Suddenly Bolan felt himself rising. The barrel was going up. This was his chance. The next moment he nearly fell off as the tank fired. The commander had an even better idea— he was going to burn Bolan off.

A ringing noise filled Bolan's ears, and he felt the barrel grow hot. Panic seized him. He pulled himself up, quickly transferred the grenade from his right hand to his left and let go of the spoon. The grenade was primed.

Another shell left the tank, the flame singeing his hair. The barrel began to heat up again. Bolan reached out and pushed the grenade into the muzzle of the cannon. A searing pain shot through his arm as his hand touched the muzzle.

The trees rushed toward him. Using all his strength to push off, he jumped, the left tread missing him by inches. He rolled and ran, stars dancing in his eyes from the blow of landing. A blast of hot air caught him from behind and sent him sprawling as the tank exploded. He hugged the ground, awaiting the secondary explosions, but nothing happened.

Bolan lifted his head. The tank burned. Flames lit the woods red. He raised himself to his feet, swayed, but managed to retain his balance. Bit by bit his hearing returned. He listened to the crackle of flames. He became conscious of the pain in his right hand. He looked at his hand, licked the burn. He stood there watching the tank, oblivious to everything. Not until the last moment did he notice the pair of headlights bumping across the field toward him.

A jeep loaded with POWs pulled up, Cosgrove at the wheel. "You hurt?" he yelled.

Bolan shook his head. "Are the trucks safe?" he asked.

"We're loading now," Cosgrove said. "The fighting is over. But we'll have to hurry. That tank managed to get off a message to Yen Sai. Eng says Hanoi has ordered the helicopter base at Tor Nok to mount a sweep first thing in the morning. They're pulling out all stops: gunships, troop inserts. They've even got parachutists standing by. Climb aboard."

A helicopter flew over. By the light of the moon Bolan caught sight of it, a strange-looking machine resembling an insect. He recognized it immediately—a Soviet-made Mi-8. The Pentagon once described it as the most heavily armed helicopter gunship in the world.

Immediately, the guerrillas near the fort opened fire and thousands of tracers filled the sky.

The gunship flew away.

But to Bolan it was an ominous sign.

THE CONVOY WEAVED CAUTIOUSLY through the night, headlights muddied over to make them invisible from the air. It was a long convoy, more than twenty jeeps and trucks. In addition to the POWs there was weaponry to be carried—mortar, rocket launchers, heavy machine guns—and the wounded.

In a radio van, fourth vehicle from the head, Bolan and Eng sat with earphones listening to the enemy's radio traffic. The air waves crackled with orders to so many units. It sounded as if the entire Vietnamese army in Cambodia was after them.

"Route seven is blocked," Eng announced.

Bolan swiveled to a map table. "Where?"

"Junction thirteen."

"That was fast," said Bolan, marking it.

"A night parachute drop," Eng said. She moved by his side. "We'll have to take this road now."

Bolan reached for his walkie-talkie. "Cosgrove."

Cosgrove rode in the lead jeep.

Bolan explained the roadblock to him. "At the next intersection we'll have to turn left."

"Let me check." A moment later Cosgrove was back. "That road leads right into Tor Nok. We'll have gunships on our tail in minutes."

Bolan looked questioningly at Eng.

"Our only chance." Eng sighed. "Or else we go on foot."

Bolan brooded at the map. Abandon the trucks. Continue on foot. On foot it would take them weeks to get out, and the longer they remained in the country the more time the enemy had to close the escape routes. The radio traffic indicated they intended to close all the routes: harbors, rivers, roads, trails, even footpaths. The Vietnamese were treating the escape as a national emergency. Fifty billion dollars was a lot of money.

"No, we can't go on foot," Bolan said.

"Or we abandon Laos," suggested Eng. "If we drive directly for Thailand we can still make it."

Bolan stared again at the map. He had no intention of abandoning the POWs in Laos. That would be compromising, giving in. No way.

"No, we can't abandon Laos."

"Then we have no choice but to take this road," Eng said.

"Do you think Cosgrove is right? That we can't drive without being spotted?"

"We'll be spotted," Eng said.

"Great," Bolan said sarcastically. He lit a cigarette and continued staring at the map. He went back to the start of the problem. Route seven was blocked. They couldn't fight their way through; the enemy would call on helicopters and make the convoy a sitting duck.

His thoughts turned to the second road, the one that led past the Vietnamese helicopter base at Tor Nok. The enemy would hear them and the helicopters would take off after the convoy. Perhaps they could destroy the helicopters. After all, they had plenty of mortar and rockets.

Destroy the helicopters? Why destroy them? No, ride them!

Ride them all the way to Laos. Maybe all the way to Thailand.

Bolan reached for the walkie-talkie....

16

The assault party jogged in the moonlight, sixty-two of the fittest POWs in the convoy. They had to be fit to be able to run with all that gear. It was a fast jog—they had only an hour of darkness left—and they were loaded down with machine guns, rocket launchers and ammunition. This was Bolan's last throw of the dice, and they were prepared for any eventuality.

As a wooded area appeared, the last before the helicopter base, Bolan waved the men down. He told them to squat while he and his two Khmer Rouge guides went ahead at a fast walking pace. They reached the woods, skirted it until they came to a footpath.

The woods were dark and silent, a thick canopy shutting out light. Fire flies flickered in the air. Slowly Bolan and his guides made their way on the path, pausing every few steps to listen for any sound of the enemy.

But it was the cigarette smoke that warned them. Someone was in the woods.

Bolan motioned his guides down. He drew his knife and continued alone, eyes probing the dark. A cigarette glowed in a clearing by the path. A listening post, he was sure of it, though he could not yet see a radio.

A listening post was better than patrols for guarding a base. Patrols made noise and could be ambushed. A listening post could detect an intruder and summon help without the intruder's knowing it—provided the guard did his job and did not smoke.

Bolan crept toward his prey, the nightfighter's suit invisible in the night, his face and hands camouflaged by dirt mixed with water.

Bolan narrowed the distance. The guard continued smoking, sitting sideways to the trail, propped against a tree.

Then something made the sentry turn in Bolan's direction. Perhaps it was his sixth sense. It took a second for his brain to catch up with his eyes and that second was fatal.

Bolan's knife left his hand. The soldier grunted and slipped sideways.

Bolan ran up to him. Open eyes stared sightlessly in the darkness. The soldier was dead. Bolan retrieved the knife, shouldered the soldier's radio and went back to his guides. He sent one to fetch the POWs.

Bolan continued through the woods with the other guide.

The POWs joined him, and he handed one the Vietnamese radio set. "If they call, pretend you're the listening post. Search the sentry's pockets so you know his name."

A minute later they came to the edge of the trees. Before them was a clear strip of land and behind that a fence. One look told Bolan it would be easy. It was a chain-link fence—and it was not electrified. "Where is the primary radio?"

"Sir." The POW carrying their own radio came up to him.

Bolan took the receiver and called Cosgrove, who was in a forest with the rest of the convoy. "We're at the perimeter," Bolan told him.

"All quiet at this end," Cosgrove replied.

Bolan turned to his men. "My team will cut the fence, the other teams cover us from the woods. Okay, let's go."

They ran across the strip and lay face down next to the fence. A POW brought out a pair of AK-47 wire cutters, which some of the mountain troops carried in place of bayonets, and started cutting. He had finished his job and was enlarging the hole with his hands when three barking dogs surged toward them. The dogs stopped by the hole and snarled, white fangs gleaming.

"Everyone stay still," Bolan said.

The POWs and the slavering animals faced off across the hole. The dogs snarled, the POWs strained their ears for the sound of handlers. But no one came. Bolan got the picture: the four-legged guards were roaming the base on their own.

"Don't you have a silenced weapon?" someone whispered.

"It went with the tank," Bolan replied.

A feeling of frustration gripped him—the escape of two hundred men held up by a trio of dogs.

"I need two fast men with bayonets, and I want a bayonet for myself."

Two young-looking men appeared. Bolan accepted a bayonet.

"Okay," he whispered. "We're going to try and take them but we've got to do it fast. Every damn time they bark it endangers our lives. I'll give the word."

The three stood, ready.

"Now!"

They moved quick as lightning, jabbing for their kill. Two dogs went down in a startled heap. One yelped. Bolan dived and helped finish it off. It was a fierce act done at great speed. The dog's snarls died in their throats, their barks frozen by the rapidity of the attack.

The animals lay in pools of blood.

They made their way past the dogs, into camp.

Bolan took the receiver from his radio man.

"Nighthawk to Cosgrove. We're inside."

Everyone resumed jogging. In the distance they could see buildings with lights. In front of the buildings helicopters were parked on a large landing zone. As they neared, Bolan recognized machines of both American and Soviet design. There were Hueys and Chinooks, Mils and Kamovs.

The man carrying the Vietnamese radio ran up to Bolan. "Sir, they're calling."

Bolan slowed down and took the receiver. A voice was calling Green two. Bolan took a handkerchief and covered the mouthpiece. A handkerchief distorted sound. "Green two," he answered.

"Where were you?" the voice asked.

"I think there's something wrong with this set."

"Report."

"Everything's quiet."

"Report in code."

"Sorry, I forgot."

"Say again?"

"I forgot the code."

"Who is this?"

Bolan turned to the man carrying the radio. "The guy's name, quick."

"Trang Dong."

"This is Trang Dong," Bolan said. An ominous silence followed. Bolan handed the receiver to the POW, and they ran to catch up with the others.

An engine burst into life on the other side of the building. It sounded like a truck. They heard it drive off, then heard it returning. A pair of headlights appeared on the strip on the other side of the fence. It was an armored car, and it was heading for the woods where Bolan had taken out the guard at the listening post.

Bolan ran to his primary radio and called Cosgrove. "Move out," he said on the run. "There may be trouble. So be prepared."

They jogged toward the buildings. Now they could make out the tower atop the air terminal—it was loaded with antennas; a communications tower. The LZ was deserted but the base was stirring. A dog barked, a door banged. The sky began turning gray. At any moment the bugle would sound the reveille.

"Number one team leader," Bolan called. A POW ran to his side. "Attack the terminal and take out that tower. We don't want them sending SOSs."

"Right, sir."

"Number two and three team leaders," Bolan continued. Two men came up. "Attack the barracks. Make sure they don't retreat toward the main gate."

The men ran off.

"Number four team leader. Secure the LZ and be ready to back up numbers two and three."

The POW with the Vietnamese radio came back. "Sir, the armored car has discovered the hole. They have orders from the base to investigate."

"Good." By the time they did, the show would be over. "Okay, men, split up."

The teams fanned out, each heading for its target, Bolan's toward the main gate. In the distance Bolan could hear the groan of engines. The convoy was coming.

A burst of gunfire hit the early morning darkness. A flare illuminated the sky. Colored tracers were flying back and forth. The battle was on.

The fifth team, with Bolan at its head, rounded the side of the terminal on the run. In front of them was a flagpost and beyond that the main gate. From a nearby guardhouse soldiers were running out. They were met by gunfire. Men fell, others retreated.

"Rocketeer!" Bolan shouted. "Guardhouse!"

The man carrying the launcher dropped to one knee. An RPG whooshed out and the guardhouse exploded in flames. The rocketeer's assistant reloaded and the group ran for the gate. It was unmanned, at least from the inside. The guards were in a sandbagged bunker outside. Before they had time to swing their machine gun around, Bolan's group was there, riddling their position.

A POW swung the gate open just as headlamps appeared on the road. The convoy! But another pair of headlights was also approaching, coming toward them on the left, racing on the strip along the side of the fence. The armored car. Bolan cursed. With its cannon, the Rhino could massacre the convoy.

"Rocketeer!" Bolan shouted again.

In the same instant Bolan realized it was impossible to shoot at the car from inside the gate. Sandbags blocked the line of fire. The rocket man would have to step out onto the strip, exposing himself to the armored car's machine gun.

"Sir?" said the rocketeer, running up to him.

Bolan grabbed the man's launcher, ran out onto the strip and knelt, the launcher over his shoulder. Tracers whizzed past him and he felt their heat. But he ignored them. Calmly he took aim.

The rocket swished out, and the car exploded in flames. But the Rhino kept on coming, bearing down on him like a fiery monster, flames belching from the hole where the turret had been. Bolan moved to the side and the car turned to follow. Bolan's calm vanished. He threw down the launcher and sprinted.

The Rhino was nearly upon him. Bolan threw himself sideways, and the armored car shot past him. It crashed into trees on the other side of the strip, and there was another explosion.

A jeep pulled up next to him. It was Cosgrove. "You're damn lucky to be alive," he said.

Bolan nodded.

On the road, trucks drove past, heading into the base. The fighting seemed to be over. The gunfire had ceased. A lot of buildings were burning. A new day was dawning.

"Where's Eng?"

"In the last truck. With the wounded."

The walkie-talkie on Bolan's gunbelt came to life. "Number four leader to Nighthawk. LZ secured. Wing commander says plenty of choppers available."

Bolan climbed into the jeep. "Air terminal."

The terminal was in shambles, bodies everywhere, the offices in flames. The tower was also burning. As they drove in, Bolan saw a couple of bullhorns with battery packs. He thought they might come in handy. Already he was thinking ahead, to Laos. He picked them up and slung them over his shoulder.

They came out onto the LZ. A helicopter lay tilted, burning. Another had lost its rotor blades, but most of the machines appeared undamaged. Groups of POWs were going from one machine to the other, inspecting them. To the side of the LZ, men from the assault force were assembling Vietnamese prisoners, making them sit down with hands on their heads.

The wing commander, the chief POW pilot, stood by a

huge Mil transport with an eight-blade main rotor. Bolan and Cosgrove approached him. He was talking to a pilot already in the cockpit. The pilot gave a thumbs-up signal, the engine whined and the blades began turning. A moment later they were spinning in a blur.

"What's the score?" Bolan shouted.

"We hit the jackpot," the wing commander replied. "They're all fueled up, ready to go. You can start loading."

Bolan turned away from the noise and brought up his walkie-talkie. "All teams, climb aboard." Then he jogged back to the air terminal to survey the operation.

A Huey gunship whined, its blades turning. A Chinook transport followed, then the Mil gunship. Chopper after chopper burst into life. Soon the air was full of throbbing blades.

17

They flew into the morning sun, skimming tobacco fields, past hundreds of sprinklers spraying water on the younger, lighter-green plants. They had been flying for three hours. Now they were nearly there—fourteen helicopters in battle formation, roaring over the quiet countryside. In the command gunship, Bolan leaned over the pilot's shoulder, watching the cluster of buildings in the distance. On his head he wore a set with an earphone and a side mike. He trailed wire to the intercom.

"The building with the tall chimneys," said Bolan. "What is it?"

"The curing center for the harvested tobacco," replied the pilot, an American POW who had been imprisoned in this camp before his transfer to Cambodia and knew it well.

"I see a lot of civilians around."

"Casual help from town. They're brought in for the picking. Do we go in shooting?"

"Definitely," Bolan said.

He reached for the channel selector and switched it from the intercom to the radio.

"This is Mil one. Here are your targets. Mil one takes out the gate, Mil two left tower, Mil three right tower. We're hoping to intimidate them, so use rockets. Four each. Fire on command."

"Anything for us?" asked a Huey pilot.

"Hueys, be ready to douse any ground fire. No rockets, only machine guns. But be careful. A lot of our men are there. Transports, no shooting unless ordered. I repeat, no shooting unless ordered."

They flew over a tractor pulling a flat trailer piled with freshly harvested tobacco leaves. On the pile sat a white man in brown overalls. At the sight of white faces in the helicopters, he began a joyful jig. Bolan waved to him.

"Chris Dunn," the pilot said. "A CIA operative captured in the Golden Triangle in eighty-three. He was working with the Montagnards in Laos."

"There wouldn't be a Colonel Wilson here by any chance?" Bolan asked.

"Never heard of him."

Too bad for Olga, Bolan thought.

The compound drew closer, and now Bolan could make out the details. A regular prison farm—the yard had buildings at one end, barracks for the POWs and garrison at the other, the two separated by a parade ground. Two flags fluttered from poles on the parade ground, the yellow star of Vietnam and the promise-of-a-bright-future white disk of Laos.

"Prepare to fire," Bolan said into his radio. They would achieve total surprise; the miradors flanking the flag-bedecked archway over the main gate were not even manned.

"Fire!"

The gunships shuddered as rockets left suspended dispensers on their sides. Bolan watched the rockets streak toward their targets. The perimeter flashed with explosions; the gate caved in; the towers collapsed like swatted stacks of cards.

The trio of Mils hedgehopped through the swirling smoke and dust. They were inside the compound, men on the ground throwing themselves down in panic. The transports followed, then the tiny Kamov, with Eng monitoring enemy communications, then the Hueys closing the rear.

They crossed the parade ground, rose and hovered above the administration buildings. The helicopters hung like angry wasps, shutting out the sun, filling the air with a continuous roar. A bullhorn blared from the command gunship.

"To the commander of the camp. You have thirty seconds to surrender or we destroy your camp."

"Nighthawk, Nighthawk!" Eng's voice called urgently on the radio. "They're sending an SOS, they're transmitting."

Bolan switched to intercom. "Where is the communications room?"

"Third floor, second window from the left," the pilot replied.

"Destroy it!"

The command gunship descended twenty feet, then moved sideways to stationary hover directly in front of the window of the targeted room.

Its twin cannon roared and the room exploded in flames and smoke. The gunship rose and returned to its position.

The fire sent men running from the building, some climbing out windows. In no time, there was a crowd in the square, hands raised over their heads. They included two white men in white safari suits.

"The white men, who are they?" Bolan asked.

"KGB," the pilot said. "They own the farm."

A figure appeared in the door of the building, a man in uniform with a cane. He stood in the dignified stance of a captain about to abandon his ship. He walked out, marched to the head of the crowd of administration workers and looked up at the command gunship. He was the camp commandant.

The bullhorn in the sky blared.

"Colonel Gia. You are requested to assemble the garrison by the flagpole with the Vietnamese flag. The troops are to lay down their arms there. You will not be harmed if you cooperate. Our sole objective is to rescue the prisoners. I await your answer."

In reply, the colonel gave a perfunctory salute. He turned to his men and issued orders. Some ran off to pass the word, others fell in step behind the colonel as he headed for the parade ground.

The bullhorn sounded again. "To all POWs. You are to assemble near the flagpole with the Laotian flag in preparation for immediate boarding. Pass the word."

"Nighthawk," Eng said.

"Yes?"

"I think the enemy heard the SOS. Radio traffic has picked up. They are using code. I know one of the code words they are using. Eagle. It means fighter aircraft."

Fighters! Bolan's insides constricted. "Thank you, Eng," he said, trying to sound calm. "Okay, guys," he went on, "you heard the lady. Let's move it. Wing commander, take over."

The wing commander issued orders for the pickup of the prisoners. A gunship carrying the second bullhorn was dispatched to tour the fields and announce the rescue.

A transport followed to make pickups in the fields.

The other transports were ordered into a holding pattern, circling the perimeter.

At word from Bolan, the gunships advanced to the

parade ground. Men were assembling near each flagpole, their numbers growing rapidly.

The POWs stood in a large loose group; the Vietnamese formed ranks with their weapons on the ground before them.

A transport broke from the circle above and touched down near the POWs. They surrounded the aircraft. Bolan could see the dispatcher shouting orders, counting men as they entered the helicopter. When his quota was up, he held up his hand, quickly slid the door shut and took off.

Another machine left the circle and touched down.

The gunships hovered, waiting, the gunners making sure the enemy did not interfere with the boarding.

The last helicopter rose from the parade ground. "All on board," the wing commander announced on the radio. It was an emotional moment.

"Let's get the hell out of here," Bolan said.

The pitch of the engines changed and the gunships moved forward. They flew out of the compound and joined the transports over the tobacco fields. The helicopters regrouped and flew west. A few minutes later they were crossing the Mekong. Now it was only twenty-five miles to the Thai border.

"Aircraft at five o'clock," a voice shouted on the radio. "Closing in fast."

Bolan knew they had two choices. They could split up, every man for himself, or stick together and try to outwit the enemy. To choose the first option was to surrender themselves to luck. The fortunate would make it, the others would go down in flames. The second option relied less on luck and more on skill. He chose the second.

"All aircraft, head back to the Mekong," Bolan said. "Change course, one three five degrees to starboard."

The flight did an about-face and Bolan could see the fighters approaching. They flew in V formation, wings glinting in the morning sunlight. The turnaround by the helicopters caught them by surprise, bypassing the fighters before they had time to react. The jets were flying west above, the helicopters flying east below.

It took some time for the fighters to backtrack. They were MiG-21s and their speed precluded a tight turn. By the time they got back to the river, the helicopters were skimming the water upstream in single file. Hills rose above them on either side. In the lead gunship, Bolan was leaning over the pilot's shoulder as they snaked their way into even higher hills.

"Let's hope the MiGs don't catch on," Bolan said.

Bolan was trying to get to Thailand by the river. Twenty miles upstream the left bank ceased being Laos and became Thailand, the river turning into the boundary between the two.

The MiGs dived out the sky, cannons blazing. On either side of the helicopters, cliffs flashed with explosions and geysers rose in the water. But all the shots went wide, the enemy unable to keep them in their sights long enough in the winding, narrow confines of the river's course. Two more attacks followed with equally dismal results. The MiGs were too fast and not maneuverable enough for the job.

But the advantage the helicopters gained was not going to last forever. The snaking river was straightening out, the hills getting smaller, the river wider. On the next attack the MiGs might start scoring.

"How long to Thailand?" Bolan asked.

"Nearly there," the pilot answered.

The last hill went by and they flew over a plain. A village

with a Thai flag passed on their left. The command gunship rose and banked to the left, the others following. A moment later they were all in Thailand. A loud cheer rose from inside the helicopters. They had made it. But the jubilation was short-lived.

"Aircraft on the port side," a voice shouted in alarm.

Bolan's pulse quickened. The MiGs were following them into Thailand. He ought to have realized they would do this—both sides were constantly violating the frontier. Should he have held off turning until they were in the mountains again? Must they go back to the river? He reached for the selector.

"It's okay, they're Thais," said the pilot who gave the alarm. "Sorry about that."

A formation of F-14s flew past, red-blue-white rondels on their fuselage. A voice with a Thai accent said on the radio. "Helicopters, identify yourselves."

"We are prisoners of war escaping from Indochina," Bolan replied.

"Welcome to Thailand, gentlemen. We've been expecting you."

"Hey, they know about us," said the pilot, beaming.

"Arrangements have been made for your reception at our former air base in Ubon," the Thai went on. "Are any of you familiar with the route?"

"We know our way to Ubon, thank you," Bolan said.

The helicopters changed course while the planes flew off. They did not fly away completely, however, but stayed in the distance. "They're making sure we don't get jumped again," said a voice on the radio.

"Yes, sir," another pilot exclaimed. "That's Thai hospitality."

They flew toward Ubon, exchanging smiles, faces flushed

with excitement. The moment the POWs had long dreamed of was about to arrive. News of a reception added to the sense of occasion. Maybe there would be a band, maybe women. For sure, there would be food and drink. But above all there would be freedom.

"What I can't understand is how they knew we were coming," said a pilot on the radio.

"They must have been monitoring the Vietnamese radio," suggested another.

The radio chatter went on. Bolan made no attempt to stop it. A holiday atmosphere prevailed.

Ubon appeared. They flew over its ocher roofs and palm-lined streets and headed for the base. It lay a few miles to the west. As they neared it, they saw a crowd near the runway. A hero's welcome awaited them.

But as soon as they touched down they got a shock. There was no band, no women. The place was stark and bare, and the people were all military policemen, some with dogs.

"I can't believe this," a voice gasped on the radio.

"You know what?" added another. "I think we're going back to jail."

18

The American prisoners marched through the base in ranks of four, flanked by Thai MPs with dogs. It was almost evening; they had spent the day in detention. They were hungry and bad-tempered, still smarting from the humiliating way they had been received.

On their arrival—before they had even stepped out of the helicopters—a bullhorn blared, ordering them to come out with hands on their heads, warning them that if they failed to obey orders they risked being shot.

Afterward they had been segregated by nationality and marched off to different buildings to be locked up. By chance, or design—in the Orient one never knew—the U.S. contingent found itself in what had been the base jail. There they were served some tasteless gruel. There, too, a guard informed them they were illegals. Now, they were on their way to learn what that meant. The guards led them into a hall arranged like an auditorium, with rows of chairs facing a table covered in green felt. Behind it sat a Thai official in a white safari suit. With an aloof air, he watched them take their chairs. When they were seated he addressed them.

"Good afternoon. I am Inspector Nakom Tan of the Thai border police. It is my task to inform you that you are under arrest for illegal entry into Thailand."

"You must be fucking joking," snapped someone in the back row.

"Our laws are no different from those in America, and the fact that you are Americans does not exempt you from them. A Mexican who enters the United States without a permit is deported, is that not so?" He let the question hang ominously. If they didn't like it, they would be sent back across the Mekong.

"The normal procedure in case of illegal entry is a trial," the official continued. "On conviction there is a fine of five thousand dollars or a five-year prison sentence followed by deportation to the place of origin. In your case, however, the authorities are prepared to waive trial on condition that you sign a plea of guilty and that your embassy pay an administrative fine of two thousand dollars per prisoner. That is to cover the cost of mobilizing our forces to arrest you." He tapped a pile of forms lying by his elbow. "The forms should be handed in to the U.S. embassy official who will address you next."

He nodded to the commander of the guards and walked out of the room. The forms were handed out.

"This is incredible," said a POW next to Bolan.

"We're getting the boat people treatment," Bolan said.

A Westerner entered the hall. It was Svenson. He caught Bolan's eye and nodded a greeting. He, too, was carrying a stack of forms. He sat down and addressed them.

"What I have to say is strictly off the record. For reasons of international politics, the U.S. government does not wish this escape to receive publicity. It might adversely affect some delicate negotiations that are under way in the area. It could also have a bad effect on the welfare of other POWs. You will therefore be asked to sign a form that I will now pass around." He signaled to the chief of the guards who repeated the procedure.

A silence descended on the hall as the men perused the

new form. It was an oath of secrecy by which the men would agree never to reveal publicly they had been POWs. Officially, they had been abroad on special assignment for the government. A note warned that those who broke the oath would be prosecuted.

"Any questions?" Svenson asked.

"What if we don't sign this form?" someone inquired.

"I don't recommend it. If you don't sign the form, the embassy will not pay your fine," Svenson replied. "You will be tried by a court and sent to a Thai jail."

"Did the other POWs sign?" someone else asked.

"Yes, they all signed."

"Where are the others?" a third man asked.

"Gone," said Svenson. "They were processed first."

Finally someone asked, "If we were government employees all this time, are we entitled to back pay?"

"Yes, you will get back pay."

"In addition to the money paid to our families?"

"Yes, the back pay is additional. I shall now read your names in alphabetical order," Svenson said. "Those who wish to avail themselves of the embassy's offer please come to the table to sign the forms. Sign both the forms I gave you and the form for the Thais. Those who do not wish to sign, kindly step through that door for processing by Thai authorities."

One by one the American POWs went up to the table and signed. No one went through the door.

When it was over, the guards took them outside and they boarded trucks. The trucks drove off for Ubon, where the men would be fed, given clothes and flown to the U.S.A.

No one said goodbye to Bolan, no one noticed that his name had not been called and that he remained inside with Svenson.

Unbearable sadness mixed with bitterness assailed Mack Bolan. He had done what he had to do, blitzed his way into the core of an international disgrace, fighting hand to hand, commanding men of many nationalities, only to find the outcome an ironic reflection of his new life—a bleak scene of cunning, wariness, loneliness.

Those he had fought to liberate were in fact no different than he in their freedom. They were equally at the mercy of forces beyond the control of the fighting man.

Bolan knew all about it. In times of danger, people love God and the soldier. When the trouble passes, God is forgotten and the soldier is slighted.

To the soldier he would say what he said to himself. Keep fighting!

Bolan and Svenson faced each other in silence, listening to the loading outside. Only when the last truck left did they speak.

"Congratulations," Svenson said. "We heard of your adventures on the Vietnamese radio. Quite a feat."

"So was yours," Bolan said.

Svenson dismissed the sarcasm with a wave of the hand. Buying people to do things, buying people not to do things, all in a day's work. He rose, gathered up the forms and put them away in a briefcase. "I have a car. Want a lift to Bangkok?"

"Where is Eng?"

"On the airstrip with Balzani. We'll stop by."

They came out of the building into the fading sunshine. In front, a shiny black limousine was idling quietly, a Thai chauffeur at the wheel. They got in and the limousine moved slowly through the empty base.

"Everyone's left," Bolan remarked.

"Yes, it's over," Svenson sighed.

"Who took care of the other POWs?"

"Their governments."

"And what about the League?"

"They'll get a refund."

"All neatly tied up."

They came onto the runway, driving past the stolen helicopters that stood where the POWs had left them, blades sagging.

At the far end of the runway, a group of people stood near a small bubble helicopter and another limousine. Among them was Eng, still wearing her bush hat.

The car pulled up and Bolan got out. There was a strange expression on Eng's face, a look he could not figure out.

Bolan nodded to Balzani, the Bangkok CIA station chief, then walked up to the Khmer Rouge captain.

"Hello, Eng," Bolan said.

She looked up into his eyes. "Will you return to Bangkok with me?" she asked.

Then Bolan read the look. It was longing, plain and simple. He realized now that she liked him more than just a friend. But he also realized they were the wrong people in the wrong time.

"I can't," he replied. "There are too many things I have to do. But I am grateful for your help. I know you had every reason in the world to refuse."

Eng swallowed and pushed the hair out of her eyes. Bolan saw a fat tear track down her cheek.

"We could never really be on the same side," Bolan continued. "And I don't mean only politically. I am not the man you think I am. Everywhere I turn, there'll be a gun trained on me, a noose hanging over my head, a bullet with my name on it."

Even as he spoke, Bolan could see a quizzical look cross her face. "It's a long story. Perhaps one day our paths will cross again, and I will tell you of my life. Goodbye, my brave friend."

Bolan leaned forward and pressed his lips to Eng's forehead, then climbed into the waiting helicopter.

The Funeral of April Rose

"And thus, in an already darkening universe, another flame has been extinguished. But the memory of that light will burn fiercely in our hearts forever. April Rose gave her life for the man she loved. She made the supreme sacrifice. And it reminds us of another sacrifice made almost two thousand years ago for the love of mankind.

"But let us try not to grieve, because we know that death is a progression of life and we were bestowed with the honor of April's presence on this earth. May God keep her.

"I shall now read to you from First Corinthians, chapter fifteen, verses fifty-one to fifty-five. 'Behold, I show you a mystery; we shall not all sleep, but we shall be changed, in a moment, in the twinkling of an eye...for the trumpet shall sound, and the dead shall be raised incorruptible, and we shall be changed.... Death is swallowed up in victory. O death, where is thy sting? O grave, where is thy victory?' "

"Mack, this is Leo Turrin. And that eulogy was read by Father Roberts, a close friend of Hal Brognola. Yes, Hal was there and so were Toby Ranger and Smiley Dublin and Tommy Anders.

"The Phoenix Force and Able Team men bore the coffin to the grave site, and they saluted as she was lowered into the ground. It was an eight-man tribute to a brave soldier.

"Toby and Smiley stood to one side, sobbing on each other's shoulders, a testament of sorrow and love for a fallen sister.

"It was very difficult for Mr. Rose to meet all of us under these circumstances. He said to me that he was glad to finally meet the faces behind the names—names that April kept mentioning each year at Christmas time when she visited him. You know, in his eyes she is still his little girl.

"Mack, we missed you. But it's just as well that your current mission kept you away. It would have been a great personal risk for you to attend the funeral. I know how strong you are, but I wonder if even you could have borne the pain of watching April's body descending into the earth forever.

"After the service ended, we all paid our respects to Mr. Rose, then everyone began to leave the cemetery. I felt I had to turn around once more and when I did, I saw April's dad standing there with his head bowed. Then he bent over and placed a single rose on the grave."

Bolan's battle-scarred hand reached toward the tape recorder. His finger hesitated only for a second, then pressed the button marked Off.

—*With thanks to reader J.N. of Pomona, California*

Readers react to the terror and the triumph!

"I read the final pages of Mack Bolan #63: *Day of Mourning* and my soul cried out in anguish, 'No!' I guess that the truest test of success for a book is whether or not it affects the reader. If that is indeed the case, then *Day of Mourning* is a success with me! Mr. Pendleton, please give us, who in our own way loved April, revenge for the betrayal and thereby a reason for April's death."

—*P.N., St. Joseph, Missouri*

"A part of me died tonight. Very few books that I've read have evoked an emotional response from me, but *Day of Mourning* was just such a book. It is undoubtedly the best Executioner book so far, despite the pain. It shows clearly that the good guys don't always win. I know Mack Bolan will kick ass for what happened, and Able Team and Phoenix Force will make some heads roll. Don, you have found the kind of writing the world wants!"

—*W.M., Todd, North Carolina*

"I would like to express my sorrow at Mack's loss of his trusted allies, Andrzej Konzaki and April Rose. April was the true equal of Mack, and she will always be remembered by me as someone who lived large, a woman who let her man do what he felt had to be done. I will miss her as much as Mack will. She was one hell of a woman and a real lady. May God take her and keep her safe until Mack and she are reunited. Again, sir, you have outdone yourself with your writing; as far as I'm concerned, yours is the best series of books ever to be written by anyone living or dead."

—*P.D., Manhattan, Kansas*

JOIN FORCES WITH MACK BOLAN AND HIS NEW COMBAT TEAMS!

Mail this coupon today!